The Ferryman and His Wife

—

The Ferryman and His Wife

Frode Grytten

—

Translated from Norwegian by Alison McCullough

ALGONQUIN BOOKS OF CHAPEL HILL
LITTLE, BROWN AND COMPANY

Algonquin Books of Chapel Hill / Little, Brown and Company
Hachette Book Group
1290 Avenue of the Americas, New York, NY 10104
algonquinbooks.com

Originally published in 2023 in Norwegian as *Den dagen Nils Vik døde* by Forlaget Oktober

Algonquin Books of Chapel Hill is an imprint of Little, Brown and Company, a division of Hachette Book Group, Inc. The Algonquin Books name and logo are trademarks of Hachette Book Group, Inc.

The publisher is not responsible for websites (or their content) that are not owned by the publisher.

The Hachette Speakers Bureau provides a wide range of authors for speaking events. To find out more, go to hachettespeakersbureau.com or email hachettespeakers@hbgusa.com.

Little, Brown and Company books may be purchased in bulk for business, educational, or promotional use. For information, please contact your local bookseller or the Hachette Book Group Special Markets Department at special.markets@hbgusa.com.

ISBN 9781643757452 (paperback) / ISBN 9781643757476 (ebook)

LCCN 2025945681

Printing 3, 2025

LSC-C

Printed in the United States of America

The Ferryman and His Wife

—

AT A QUARTER PAST FIVE in the morning Nils Vik opened his eyes, and the last day of his life began. He lay there somewhere between dreaming and waking, sure that he would slip back into sleep, as was his habit. But now the day was here. He turned over, becoming aware of the room, the clock radio, the cold drifting in through the open window. There were no bloodstains on the pillow today, as far as he could see. What had he been dreaming about? A hand through his hair, fingertips brushing his cheek, a voice that reached him through the darkness. *I'll wait for you downstairs, sweetheart.*

He set his feet on the cold floor, went into the bathroom, pulled down his pyjama bottoms and emptied himself of the weight of the night's piss, which poured into the toilet bowl in a single, long sigh. He began to do what had to be done. He was still capable of performing his morning ritual with efficient movements: get himself upright, find clothes, make coffee, eat breakfast, go down to the boat whatever the weather. These movements, drilled into him over the course of a long life.

In the shower he watched the water as it gushed over his pale skin. At the sink he dragged his razor across his cheeks and jaw, down his throat and over his Adam's apple. His right hand was trembling slightly – he had to be careful. He didn't want to cross the fjord with a plaster on his upper lip or a bloody scrap of toilet paper stuck to his chin. What else? Teeth? Hands? Pomade? He considered omitting the aftershave. But this day couldn't be any different to yesterday, or the day before that, or any other day before that one.

The man in the mirror. A man of medium height, stocky and strong; hair once dark but now streaked with grey. A deeply furrowed face, high forehead, narrow eyes, brows that could do with a trim. Gravity had played its part; he would often joke that only his feet still looked like their full and true selves. He held his own gaze. The man in the mirror stared back at him, lowered his arms, attempted a smile. He was a man who liked to know everything about what went on around him: the weather, the wind, the tides. He was now looking at a man who no longer knew where he was going.

A stream of voices came rushing through the air and up the stairs. Nils made his way down to the kitchen, where one of the chairs caught his attention. There was a small indentation in the seat cushion, a depression he couldn't remember having seen before, as if someone had broken in during the night and was now waiting for him. Otherwise, everything appeared as it always did. The humming of the refrigerator, the dirty plates in the sink.

A voice was prattling on, somewhere in the house. Nils turned, and followed the sound. The transistor radio stood in the hallway, he must have left it there with the volume turned up late last night. He took the radio back into the kitchen with him. What day was it? A peaceful, rainy day in November. The voice on the radio reported that the weather would clear up later, there might even be some sunshine. A deer had fallen onto a speeding car beside the fjord. A missing boy had been found by the police in the city. A fire had broken out aboard a ferry.

Nils made coffee, poured himself a cup and stirred in two lumps of sugar. Still sleepy, he spread a slice of bread with syrup, but then sat there frowning at it. His stomach trouble meant that every meal now felt tedious and pointless. He stared into the living room as he chewed and swallowed each bite of bread, aided by small sips of the coffee. The old furniture was heavy and dark, as if it would stand here for all time. Three generations had passed through these rooms, fluttering around like insects, filling each floor with the sounds of life and joy.

They were still on the walls and in the frames on the dresser, these photographs from baptisms and confirmations, weddings and other days that had passed before this last one. He had lived his whole life here, first with his mother, father and brother, later with his wife and two daughters. He didn't know what would happen to the house after he was gone. He had spoken to Eli and Guro during the summer, had sat them down at the kitchen table and told them they'd have to agree on who would have what. He wanted no arguments about their childhood home after he was gone – he had seen far too many siblings exchange their parting words at a parent's funeral. His daughters had laughed it off. They had joked and smirked, but they had promised there would be no arguing.

Nils turned, reached for the kitchen drawer and took out a pen and a postcard. The card featured an image of the fjord on a summer's day, with sunshine and fine white clouds above the mountains. In an unsteady hand, he wrote a brief greeting across the sky, then propped the card against his coffee cup. What would the girls think when they found it? Would they smile? Would they cry? *I have left this house, and I won't be coming back. Take good care of each other. Dad.*

After listening to the news at six-thirty, he stood and said thanks for his meal. He had continued to do this even after his wife had died. Thank you, Marta, he said, and looked over at the kitchen chair that had once been hers. When she was alive, she would lean across the table after they had finished eating, place her hand over the back of his, give it a gentle rub and say, You're welcome.

He went outside to pick up the newspaper. His last newspaper. It was limp from lying out in the rain. *Rescued alive after an hour in the deep,* read the front-page headline. There was also an image of a footballer under the heading: *Dream Debut.* Should he sit down to read it? No, this last newspaper would remain unread. He went down into the cellar and set it atop one of the many piles. This was how it had to be, he had to do this right, make sure even the very last newspaper was in its proper place. People were surprised if they accompanied him down to the cellar and saw the bundles of newspapers there. All those days, all those years, all the lost time stacked here, all the way back to when he'd been given the job. He was once the man who delivered the newspaper to people along the fjord; he had brought them wars, fires, murders, weather forecasts, election results, football results, special offers on cars and suits and televisions.

We can't have the cellar so full of the past, Marta had said.

Can't we?

No. And anyway, it's a fire hazard.

Such is life, Marta.

She didn't say it out loud, but Nils knew that Marta longed to get rid of the newspapers that landed on every chair and rug and tabletop before they eventually fluttered down to the cellar. She didn't care for the printer's ink that marked their tablecloths and clothes; she said that even the living-room wallpaper had been dirtied by it. Nils had replied that it would have been lovely had the pattern on the wall been created by the great and small happenings out there in the world, but he was sure the marks were from his hair oil. If he was especially tired after a night out on the fjord, he might lean against the wall beside the door and sleep standing up, the way horses do. They had tried to remove the marks, but all the washing had only made them worse; they expanded, like maps of an unknown continent.

Nils considered whether there was more to be done in the house. Were there things he should take with him? What do you take with you when you know you're not coming back? He took the Omega from the corner cabinet and saw that its hands had stopped a little after ten o'clock on the nineteenth of some forgotten month. He wound up the watch and set the time. A quarter to seven? The eighteenth of November? The nineteenth? No, the *eighteenth*, of course. The watch had been a gift from Marta on their silver wedding anniversary. She had spent a lot of money on it, and she'd been hurt when he had continued to wear his old one every day. He had explained that he didn't want to scratch the glass; his work didn't permit him to wear such a nice watch.

He went back up to the bedroom, stripped the bed and heaped all the bedding into a loose pile. Then he lifted the mattress out of its frame and jostled the ancient thing over to the landing. He wrestled the mattress down the stairs and through the hallway before he put on his shoes, managed to open the front door, and shoved the mattress out onto the gravel. He had matches and paraffin at the ready, and he dragged the mattress a short distance from the wall of the house before he set it alight. Every six months, he and Marta had carried the old mattress out into the garden to remove the smell of sleep from it and breathe new life into its tired, worn fibres. When they put the mattress back in the frame, they made sure to always turn it over, so they would spend six months lying on each of its sides.

The mattress smouldered for a while before the flames took hold of its stained surfaces. Nils Vik stared at the dark rings of blood, yellow blooms of urine, breastmilk stains and decades of semen and sweat, fragments of skin and hair and nails, traces of jam and coffee and breakfasts in bed every birthday, hopes and joys he had forgotten and which would now go up in smoke. He even thought he glimpsed the imprint of her body, where she had lain like an S on her side of the bed, but it must have been his imagination. The mattress told the story of an entire life. It felt too private to allow other people – and even *complete strangers*, for all he knew – to deal with their past. Nils went back up the front steps, and turned to see the mattress ablaze on the gravel.

A LITTLE AFTER SEVEN, Nils Vik walked through the house for the last time. The floorboards creaked beneath his feet; the handrail on the stairs felt cool against his palm. He put on a wool sweater, found his peacoat, picked up his cigarettes and took his skipper's cap from the hook. He rummaged through his pockets for his keys, and eventually found them.

He went into the living room and sat down on the sofa. This was a habit he had acquired – the journey was always better, he felt, if he sat for a while before heading out. If he simply sat there, in the peace and quiet. Thinking things through. Clearing his head. This morning he was afraid he might remain sitting there, that he would lose the motivation to go down to the boat. He was ready to leave; he wanted to stay. He stood, and his heart began to pound. The last time he had been to see the doctor, he'd been told that his heart was impaired. In a serious voice, the doctor had said he was worried about Nils's heart. What a farce, to spend all that time on a diagnosis Nils himself could have made instantly.

He stood outside on the front steps for a moment. From the house he could hear whispering and sighing, the low voices, the arguments, the radio with its fishing report. The footsteps and the humming, the flushing of the toilet. Marta playing cards with the girls, the gurgling of the coffee machine, doors being opened and closed. He took out his keys, about to lock up, but then went back inside to get the radio and his hip flask. Then he turned on the outdoor light he had just switched off. It was Marta who had insisted that a light be kept on, an outdoor light that would shine through the night. So Nils could navigate and find his way home should he run into problems out on the fjord. He had stuck to it. No reason to change it now. There would always be a light on in this house.

The day had yet to take on its colours. The grass was trampled flat and autumnally mottled, and it had stopped raining. He loved mornings like this, laden and untouched, with milky fog drifting down the mountainsides. To walk to the boat, stand at the wheel, light a cigarette and watch its ember flicking up and down. A shadow came into view down on the gravel road, and out of the dim, grey light came Luna. The dog jumped up at him, twisting and thrashing, whining and wagging.

Ahaha! Luna cried. Here I am! Down here! Here!

Nils couldn't help but laugh. Where on earth had the dog come from? From the other side? From the next world? How many years had it been since she had run into the road only to be mown down by a passing truck? Twenty? Twenty-five? She used to sit patiently in the wheelhouse, staring out at the waves and the rain and the lights along the fjord. Then at some point the dog had started talking, commenting on people and events and the weather. What a guy! Luna might say. She's not quite right in the head, that one, Luna might say. Lovely day, though, isn't it? Oh, the things the two of us have seen and done, Nils!

He soon found he could talk to Luna about anything and everything – about boats and planes and politics and football. Now she was walking obediently at his feet once again, playful and happy, following every step he took towards the water and the boathouse, where he pushed the warped window closed from the outside before he opened the door. Hello? he called softly into the darkness, inhaling the scent of diesel and rotten fishing nets. He had thought she might be waiting here, but when he turned on the light, he saw that he was alone.

Nils went over to the window he'd just closed and secured the catches from the inside. He had received several offers to buy the boathouse – the entire plot, in fact – but he had told the estate agents and developers in no uncertain terms that it wasn't for sale. Aren't you going to sell, Nils? his neighbours had asked. All of them had sold. The bay was now full of cabin people, city people who had forced their way right down to the water's edge, the kind of people who would convert the boathouses' interiors, secretly redecorate, and then apply to the local council for a change of use. One fine day that roof's going to come down on your head, Nils! people said. Just look how the water pours in when it rains! But his boathouse stood. Everything was getting older, everything was in decline, everything was made to fall apart. But his boathouse stood.

Their elder daughter had been conceived here, over in the corner, under a roof that had rested heavily above their heads. He remembered the falling rain, he remembered his trousers around his knees and Marta giving a running commentary on the sperm cells swimming inside her only to seep out again. Do you think one of them will make it? she had asked. And that was how Eli was made. Had it really happened? Or was it simply something he clung to as part of the story of their lives? Yes, it had happened, but you can never know for certain with these things. He took a hammer and pliers from the tool shelf and removed two links from the Omega's steel wristband. He must have got thinner since he last wore the watch, yes, he was wizened now, and more fragile. He found lubricant and his oilskins, greased the slam-shut lock on the door, and heard how it shunted closed behind him for the very last time.

The tide was on the ebb this morning – it was a calm day, but not still, for the fjord is never still, it rumbles and rustles, it whispers and rushes, even on days with no wind. All the sounds he recognised, all the noise and hubbub he had learned to read and interpret. He climbed down the ladder and stepped over into the boat, his body weaker and stiffer now, yet still with enough agility to make it safely across. Luna lingered a little on the quay, turning several circles around herself and hopping lightly from foot to foot before she risked it and leapt over onto the deck.

Which boat was it? The MB *Marta*, of course – a boat that had served him well, a boat he had purchased just after the war, full of optimism and belief in the future. It was a boat that could handle the sea, which could withstand the wind and the waves. A boat made of oak, 36 feet long, 9 feet wide, painted white with red stripes on her hull and cabin. An elegant sailboat he had de-rigged to put in a

12-horsepower combustion engine, which he later replaced with an inboard diesel. He'd added the cabin and wheelhouse, and it had taken fourteen months to convert the sailboat into a ferryboat.

He turned the key in the ignition. The motor started on the first try, as it always did, no matter the weather. Cylinders came to life; pumps began to work; intense heat ignited atomised fuel. The smell of diesel rose from the engine bay, like aromas in a kitchen, and the wheel began to vibrate gently between his hands. He listened to the knocking and thudding, the most comforting sound in all the world. This heart, with its strong, ropy muscles, which for all these years had worked beneath him.

OVER THE FJORD HE GOES. Over the fjord without hesitation. Over the fjord, like so many times before. Late and early, morning and evening. Through storm or stillness, east and west. Only the gulls follow him: they mutter and complain, seeming unnaturally white as they hang there above the boat. The only human traces this morning are the light from the house and the headlamps of a car working its way down the fjord's western side.

Nils Vik turns around. He thinks he can see a column of smoke rising up beside the house, the mattress must be consumed by now, reduced to ash. Almost immediately, the house begins to slip out of sight. The next time he turns, he won't be able to see it. All his minutes exist in that house, all his hours, all his days. After all these years he has learned that a good home is a fortification, a cocoon surrounding the body, a shelter that comes after skin and clothes. To be there, make food, make babies, sleep. To wake, to eat, to piss and shit and love.

It is almost seven-thirty. It's morning, yet still night, the darkness retained within all the bedrooms, people sleeping with duvets pulled up around them. Soon they'll make breakfast, soon they'll head out to the barn to tend to the animals, soon they'll start the milking machines, they'll check nets and fish corrals, drive to football matches and family dinners. Bells will summon congregations to church services, their peals trembling on the water's surface. Time

13

has outrun him. It's been a matter of time for a good while already. It is always a matter of time. On this last day he will pull a thread through time, follow it backwards, see where time takes him. He will travel this fixed route, or rather the *scheduled routes*, for the very last time. He will trace what he has loved in life, lift it up, honour it. For if *he* doesn't do this, who will?

Oh, Luna says, casting a glance at Nils.

She says *oh*, softly, a couple more times, little more than sighs in the wheelhouse. The boat sits steady in the water now, creating small bow waves as they sail across its dark and mysterious surface. Nils doesn't turn, he doesn't turn, doesn't turn, only stares through the window.

Oh, Luna says again.

Shut it, Nils says.

Said nothing! says the dog.

How does one know? The bloodstains that spot the pillow? The shade of pink in the toilet bowl? It's impossible to know. He's just surprised that, thus far, this last day has been like all the others. He has risen from the same bed, has eaten his usual breakfast, has sauntered down to the old boat. Now he's out on the same fjord, a tiny blip in the landscape, with everything about to stretch out before him.

Luna stares at him with eyes like two wet question marks.

What do you remember best, Nils? she asks.

I don't know.

So much is lost to him, so much is gone, an absence that will soon encompass everything. He'll have to check the logbooks, surely they're still here somewhere? Yes, there they are. Small blue logbooks, one after the other, around twenty-five in total. How often he has stared into space, deep in thought, before scribbling down a few lines. He's even cut off the fingertips of his right glove to better grip his pen. What did he feel was worth noting? The weather, of course. Politics, geography. He's drawn doodles and copied out quotations from the newspaper, created squad line-ups and fixtures. He's written down the fares he took, a small red ring circling each amount.

He has created this little waiting room in time for people, and yes, he's even ferried sheep and goats across. All kinds of people have squeezed in here with him, for a few minutes, a few hours. Then they would step ashore and disappear, disperse, these people destined for so many different places. He got them to the city, to the doctor, the priest and the midwife, he got them to school and to funerals. Nils's boat was a fragment of their existence, a brief pause in their daily routine. But to him the boat was much more, this boat that became a way of life. His boat tore along these waters, it hummed and sang and swayed. The boat was a satellite, a moon that orbited the fjord.

So what do *you* remember best? Nils asks.

Me? Luna replies, settling her snout atop her paws.

Our walks in the forest, she says, after pondering for a moment.

I don't remember us walking in the forest.

Oh, but we did. We loved being in the forest. Loved it.

But when were we ever in the forest?

All dogs like being in the forest. No matter whether we've been there or not. The pine cones! The sticks! Oh, the sweet smell of wet bark!

What does he remember best? Yes, now he knows. Coming home late at night or early in the morning, home to the house in Vika after having been out in the wind and the waves. Tiptoeing across the floor so as not to wake those who had long since fallen asleep. Turning off the light, leaving only the single outdoor lamp burning. Sitting in the darkness in the kitchen with a dram, looking down at his hands and thighs, looking at the tattoos on his forearms, at all the surfaces. Being somewhere between night and day, between dozing and waking. Being dead tired, being alive, having eyes that see only in monochrome after being open for so long. The nights when Marta hears his footsteps in the gravel, his boots crossing the frozen grass or tramping over the compacted snow – she's such a light sleeper, on the nights he's out on the fjord she sleeps so lightly, listening to the branches of the trees that move and scrape against the walls of the house, attuned to every sign of a change in the weather. The nights when she comes down to him, her cardigan over her shoulders. When she comes up behind him as he sits there, shot glass in hand. The nights when she puts her arms around him.

A SICKLY LIGHT SETTLES OVER them now, giving definition to forms and shapes. Nils Vik grips the wheel and closes his eyes, then opens them again. Is that the dead coming through the openings in the forest? Yes, here they are. Here they come. The dead surge forth, just as the day is about to surge forth. The dead become clear, become manifest in the grey that reigns between eight and nine o'clock on a November morning.

Look, Nils says.

What? Luna asks.

There, Nils says, and points towards land.

The dead must have gathered in the forest, they must have found each other, these lonely souls who no longer belong to anyone, who have left everything they love behind. They come through the fields and down the mountainsides, they walk out onto steep cliffs, onto the smooth, coastal rock. Once there, they stand still.

Nils slows the boat and steers closer to the western side. The hum of the motor quiets, the boat almost scrapes against the shore. The dead are just metres away now, filled with the morning's languidness. They stand apart, but they must have tainted each other, for they have become almost a single creature, one being. They stand silent and still, but they are alive. They belong to the past, but they exist here and now.

You can turn back, Nils – you do know that, don't you? Luna asks.

No, he replies. No, I can't go back.

Are you sure?

Yes, I can't turn back now.

They are a hallucination, they must be, but Nils doesn't know if he can leave them, or shake them off. Have the dead come to him? Or have they come from him? Do they want to come aboard, do they wish to join him? Nils studies each and every face. Marta is not among them.

But here they come, yes, here they are. All his passengers – they ooze out of the logbooks, arise from his handwriting, grow out of his memory. They line the fjord, they are with him, they present themselves in the hope of being recognised. See us. Touch us. Speak of us.

Who were his very first paying passengers? That's right – Synnve and Sverre Nesbø on 5 May 1948, a breezy Saturday with few clouds, a lovely spring day, it says in the logbook. And did he not see the Nesbøs just now? Were they not there among the dead? Indeed – a man and wife who had ground each other down, as married couples often do, often begrudgingly and with catastrophic results. Out on the fjord that day in May 1948, Nils Vik had realised that this couple were on their very first outing to the city together. As they approached the city fjord, Sverre Nesbø said straight out that he was against the whole trip, there was too much clearing, chopping, milking, shovelling and slaughtering that needed doing at home. His wife snorted, and said the apple tree would most likely still be standing when they got back, and the cows, too – yes, even the house and the hay barn, the whole lot would still be there, guaranteed!

Once safely disembarked, the couple had made their way up the main thoroughfare, arm in arm, then vanished onto the city streets. Nils had sat out on the deck that day, smoking and enjoying a dram as he studied the people who buzzed past. Sverre Nesbø returned quickly, declaring that city life wasn't for him – he'd had to look four or five times just to cross the street, all kinds of people had bumped into him, he hadn't had a moment's peace. His wife, on the other hand – she wanted to try on clothes, she wanted to taste pastries and look in shop windows.

I gave her two hours, Sverre Nesbø said. If she isn't back by four o'clock, then she's made her choice.

And what choice is that? Nils asked.

Then she's chosen city life.

The pair of them passed the time by playing cards, and Nils treated his passenger to a nip of whisky. At around three-thirty, Sverre Nesbø asked Nils if he could bum a cigarette; he began to stride back and forth on the quay in his slightly shabby suit. At two minutes to four, Synnve Nesbø came back down the main thoroughfare, smiling and carrying a bouquet of roses. At that point Nils had been instructed to start the boat's motor and put out.

You spent my money on *flowers*? Sverre Nesbø asked.

Your money? his wife asked in return.

Yes, mine.

What an idiot of a man I married, Synnve said, and jumped aboard.

THIS IS HOW HIS LAST DAY begins. Standing at the wheel, listening to the past and listening to the radio, the November sky above him and the motor humming below, the logbooks open. At Kviene he passes a pleasure boat with its lanterns lit. Nils can't see the other boatman very clearly, but he can just make out a man and a dog. The guy waves and says hello as the boats pass each other. Nils doesn't wave back. People who go around saying hello out on the fjord can't be taken seriously. It's as if they don't know what can happen on the fjord or out at sea. They can't possibly have seen a boat go down, or have heard the sound of one ship hitting another: *KRANNNG*. You have to keep a cool head, you have to concentrate. Nils has often thought that boatmen who go around saying hello to people must feel vulnerable and lonely, but standing there waving your arms isn't exactly much use. *Ahoy there! Here I am! Such an idiot!*

I have a good boat, he would say whenever Marta implored him to learn to swim. He said the most important thing was to have a boat you could trust, and he had such a boat. Not even the foulest weather could get the better of his boat.

The beautiful thing about his boat was how everything worked. Indeed, the higher the waves rose, the safer he felt. You're forgetting what happened to your father,

Marta said. The fjord giveth and the fjord taketh away, he'd replied then. It was his nature, he was a man of the fjord, a ferryman. He had patiently explained how the word *ferje* – ferry – came from Old Norse. That ferry actually means *fare* – danger – and if he drowned, that was just how it was. You're a fool, Marta had said. Not much to be done about that, had been his reply. Generations of seafarers had never learned to swim. If their boats went down, it was game over regardless. It was best to drown quickly. Swimming only prolonged the suffering.

One winter morning, after Nils had made his way home in unusually rough waters, Marta was waiting for him down on the quay. She stood there with Nils's overcoat wrapped around her, her hair whipping in the wind, and as he hopped ashore he saw how swollen her face was. Nils had been about to pull her to him, to embrace her, but she grabbed hold of his peacoat and shook him with a strength he didn't know she possessed. Then she swung at him with her clenched right fist. He was so surprised that at first he began to laugh, but then the pain shot through his skull, and he felt the blood running from his nose and mouth.

Marta hit him again. And then again. She began to pepper him with blows to his face and torso. Nils stumbled, almost losing his balance; like a boxer on the defence, he raised his hands to shield his face. Marta didn't let up. He tried to pin her arms to her sides, but she wriggled free and kept swinging. In the end he fell to his knees, grabbed hold of the coat she was wearing and clung to it as he begged her to stop.

You have two daughters, you have me, you have an entire family, she said. You will learn how to swim.

The day is still swaddled in morning mist. As they pass Sandøy, it looks as if the island is about to free itself from the water and sail down the fjord. When was he last out there? Didn't he go swimming on Sandøy this past summer? He went swimming there the previous summer, at any rate. That summer had been something truly special, one fine day after the next – good Lord, they'd had no choice but to throw themselves into the water to cool off. Yes, he had gone swimming there this past summer, too. He remembers taking the boat and swimming off the island on that last beautiful summer's day.

At the time, he hadn't known it would be the last day of summer, or that it would be his last swim. Only now can he say this with certainty. Perhaps his swimming trunks are still hanging from one of the island's pine trees, he's pretty sure he can recall forgetting them and considering going back. Over the years, he has learned to enjoy swimming. Marta had to force him into the water those first few times. It's freezing cold, he complained. Yup, and it won't get any warmer, she said. Marta had called him a wimp and a scaredy-cat and a chicken; she had teased him and coaxed him. Don't let go of me, Nils said as he thrashed around, floundering. I won't, she said. If you let go of me, I'll kill you, he said. I won't let go of you, she said. Just keep your head above water, relax your body. Slowly, he had begun to enjoy it. Jumping out into the water, feeling that cold shock, taking a few long strokes, permitting the slow movement to spread from his fingers all the way down to his toes. There was nothing lovelier than chugging out to Sandøy with Marta and the girls, on Sundays when the heat had settled over land and sea. Taking off his T-shirt and sandals, taking a deep breath and diving below the surface, swimming over to his girls' shimmering legs, tickling them and then resurfacing, grinning, to hear their desperate shrieks. Swimming with his girls clinging to his neck and back, getting out and shaking off the water the way Luna used to, swimming and getting hungry before dinner and crossing the fjord to buy ice cream from the store.

All these last times. The end is never as you imagine it, and the end is everything, is it not? There will be a last time you swing your daughter onto your shoulders and carry her through the forest. A last time you walk up the mountainside and gaze out across the landscape that is yours. A last time you go to the store to buy bread and milk and butter. A last summer. A last swim. He had floated on his back over there in August, looking up at a blue sky and the white clouds that had been chalked across it. He had sat on the warm, smooth rocks, closed his eyes, and listened to the gurgling of the fjord.

IT'S LUNA WHO SEES the boy with the guitar first. She sets her paws against the windowpane, scratching at it. Look! she says. There, over there!

They've made it down to Bu now, and it's nine-thirty. Yes, it has to be the boy with the guitar. Who else would be sitting on the quay smoking a cigarette on a Sunday morning? The boy is sitting in the exact same spot as when they had first collected him, one cold and snow-filled January morning in 1971.

Shall we go over there and pick him up? Nils asks.

Yes! Yes! Luna replies.

Nils slows the boat and heads for the shore.

The boy stands there as he used to, breathing warmth into his hands and grinning as Nils manoeuvres the boat alongside the quay. His hair is still long. He still has his guitar case with him. He's still sixteen or seventeen. Luna dashes out onto the deck once the boy has stepped aboard, she licks his neck and chin as if he's a treat, the dog is so giddy that in the end the boy tumbles over.

You sure took your time, says the boy with the guitar.

Oh, stop your whining, says Nils.

He laughs and embraces the boy, pulling him close.

The school headmaster had said that Jon Anderson was a real troublemaker, someone everyone was growing tired of, someone people just couldn't take any more of. Nils had agreed to have the boy aboard for a few weeks, a few months, depending on how things went. Jon had said hardly a word on their first few trips, it took a week before he loosened up. One morning he'd turned up with a black eye. Who beat you up? Nils asked. The others, the boy replied. Why? Well, I mean, why not? Another morning, four bloody dots had marked the back of his hand. Who stuck their fork in you? Nils asked. My father, the boy replied. How come? Oh, I dunno – bad table manners, maybe?

After those first silent trips it had been like having an extra radio on board – they could switch the boy on in the morning and then they'd have sound for the rest of the day. If it was just the three of them, the boy and Nils and Luna, he would play guitar for hours. Jon Anderson played songs he couldn't possibly understand, songs full of hopes and dreams. And when he wasn't playing his guitar, he would balance on the gunwale with his arms spread wide, or jump ashore to search for birds' eggs among the pines. Nils has written in the log book: *That's also one of life's phases, no gravity, no peace, there every morning with his skinny limbs and feral spirit.*

It's good to see you, Nils says.

Can't really say the same, the boy grins.

So how are things?

Good – if you ignore the fact that I'm, like, dead.

Nils says the boat's cabin still bears traces of the boy's shenanigans – he should go right on in and see for himself. Jon looks confused, so Nils reminds him of the letters carved into the woodwork. When the boy was bored, he would etch the names of his favourite bands into the wood with his pocketknife. Nils had bellowed himself blue when he'd discovered the damage.

I didn't take good enough care of you, Nils says.

You were the only one who did take care of me, says Jon.

One autumn day in 1971, Nils Vik had been summoned to the Anderson family home. For what reason he didn't know until he knocked on the front door and the boy's father opened it. There was no mistaking him. White shirt, Sunday-best trousers. Sombre, simple-minded.

He was invited in. Jon stood in the hallway; he gave a brief nod in Nils's direction. Jon's mother, who was waiting in the living room, said nothing. Nor did she make any gesture of greeting, she simply went out to fetch coffee and biscuits. Anderson asked Nils to take a seat. The chair's worn armrests suggested someone had sat there in it, patiently, for a long time. Above the television set hung an image of Jesus, along with one of the king. Jon's father said that in spite of being the man who put the household's food on the table, he was the last to know about all kinds of goings-on. He looked at his son.

And now she tells us she wants to quit school.

She? Nils asked.

Yes – that's a girl, isn't it?

No, not that I can see.

Well, as far as I'm aware, only girls have long hair. Regardless, she's disappointed us all.

Your boy hasn't disappointed me – not for a single day has he disappointed me. So why am I here?

Because there's always a risk a man might lose his self-control. You're my insurance that what's about to happen remains above board.

Anderson said education was essential – by going to school a person had a chance to make something of themselves. He was under the impression that his child had recently grown close to a responsible adult, which of course was only positive, but he and his wife wondered whether the ferryman might have been putting certain ideas into their child's head.

I'm afraid you'll have to ask your son about that – it's his choice.

No – until she's of age, we're the ones who decide.

Anderson asked his wife to go and fetch the scissors, a comb and a towel, then slipped out to the kitchen and returned with a spindle-back chair, which he set in the middle of the room. There was nothing wrong with girls, he said, as he arranged the towel over the chair's back. Quite the opposite, in fact – if they'd actually had a daughter, she would have been welcomed just as warmly as any son. But alas, they had had a son, and it was high time he stopped gallivanting around like some long-haired sissy.

Anderson gestured towards the stool with a hand. *Please, sit.* Jon only stood there with a smirk on his face, his arms crossed.

The father turned to Nils.

Well, since she refuses to listen to her own father, perhaps you might be so kind as to pass on the message that she sit down.

Don't you dare ask anything of *him*, the boy said.

Sit down, the father said.

No, said the son.

Sit.

No.

Anderson cleared his throat and began to pull his belt from the waistband of his trousers. Once that was done, he pointed at the chair again. The hand in which he held the belt was squeezed white with anticipation. Nils thought the father seemed to exude a kind of glee at the prospect of giving his own son a good hiding.

Nils stood up.

You do realise it's a criminal act to use force on another person? he said. Even if that person is a member of your own family?

Well, at least somebody is finally telling me *something*, the father said.

Again, he pointed at the chair. His son sneered.

Sit down, the father said.

Go to hell, said Jon.

What did you say?

I said: *Cunt.* You motherfucking cunt.

We do not use that kind of language in this house.

Yes we do. I do.

The father stepped closer to his son, so close that they stood just centimetres apart. Nils forced himself between them, his back to the boy and his face to the boy's father. He looked at Anderson and thought he could practically hear the man's brain shaking in his skull. Anderson took a

28

step to the right, away from Nils, then ordered his son to sit down. The boy refused, also taking a step to the side. Nils put himself between them again. Anderson repeated the movement – this time to the left. And so they continued in this strange dance, to the right, to the left, and back again. Finally they all stood in their original positions, as if frozen.

You so much as lay a finger on him, Nils said, and I'll cripple you for life.

The father stared at Nils, his breathing ragged, chest heaving, eyes burning, his face plum-red with rage. Then the man spat, sending a gob of phlegm straight into Nils's face. It took Nils by surprise, but he simply wiped it away and stood face-to-face with the man, staring him down, waiting in what had now become a wordless confrontation. The father continued to stand there for a while, then staggered backwards slightly, as if he suddenly felt dizzy. He sat down on the chair he himself had set out, bending over and clutching his stomach with both hands. The boy took a few steps towards his father and held out a hand. His father gazed at the outstretched limb, half confused, half disgusted.

Give him the scissors, the mother said. Just give him the scissors, Gabriel.

The father surrendered the scissors to his son and stared down at the floor. It was as if another man sat there now, a stranger in this living room, a man who all at once had been set adrift, left behind. A brief sound escaped his throat, almost like a mourning cry, or the whimper of a sleeping child.

Nils has lost count of how many times he's returned to this moment, the evening on which he realised a family's dynamic can be turned on its head in a matter of seconds. Suddenly it was the father who was on the outside, the aging father who was being punished, who was weaker, who suffered. A man who would never again be able to force his way back into his family with threats of violence.

So what happened to you? Nils asks. Jon grins and asks if he can bum a cigarette. He flicks the lighter, inhales, blows out smoke. Come on, what happened? What happened? He stole his father's car, a 1963 Opel Rekord. A real piece of junk – that car had made all kinds of noises, *weird* noises – you'd hear it when driving at speed, or just after turning off the engine, a strange knocking. It was the kind of car you just knew was going to crash, sooner or later.

How fast were you going? Nils asks.

Dunno – a little over a hundred, maybe? the boy says. I thought I could drive as fast as I liked.

It was a night in spring. The road was empty of other vehicles; the headlights jumped and swerved in time with the car's movements, the breeze blasted his face and chest. Jon's lover was in the car with him. The two of them had just got together, and they'd decided to get out of town, as quickly as possible. A car came towards them, Jon says, with its headlights still on full beam – he braked, they skidded sideways, and then the road was ripped out from under them. The Opel flew over and out and down; the radio died the instant they hit the fjord; water began to surge over the bonnet and windscreen. The pair were trapped. As the water seeped into the car and his mouth and lungs, Jon grasped his lover's hand. What a heavenly way to die, he had thought, to die by his lover's side as the car slowly filled with fjord.

Yeah, that was fine by me, the boy says. Totally fine.

Nils says he attended Jon's funeral, that he had watched as the white coffin was lowered into the ground on that fine day in May. He had wanted to offer his condolences, to show sympathy, but Jon's father had ignored Nils's outstretched hand and instead looked straight through him. His face was red and puffy. The man had spat on Nils's shoes and walked on. Nils had also assisted in pulling up the wreck. He'd had to turn his face away when the deceased came into view. He'd caught a glimpse of Jon in the driver's seat, his head thrown back and his shirt open, hand-in-hand with his lover. In the glove compartment was a .38 revolver with an empty chamber.

What was the revolver for? Nils asks.

It was just in case, Jon says.

In case of what?

In case anyone tried to stop us.

CROWS SIT ON THE TELEPHONE lines up ahead. The crows are like water, the crows are constant and eternal, a permanent feature of this landscape. They chatter and screech as in ancient times. Ca-ca-can you co-co-come? Ay-ayyy, wh-wh-what will be-co-co-come of that? Br-br-bring meee a-a-a b-b-boat. After they'd had a telephone installed in the house – a black crank-wind that could be used to contact the operator, with an extra-large cradle so it could hang upright on the wall in the downstairs hallway – people had called round the clock. Riiing-riiing. Riiing-rii-ing. Hell-oooo! Heee-lloooo! Oh, hell-ooo! Ye-eees, are you co-co-coming? The crows cawed up there on the telephone wires, they dropped down to the ground, hobbled around, flapped their wings. They needed help, they needed a boat, they needed him. They were his eternal headache. They were a pest and a plague. Uff-fff. A-a-are you o-o-on your wa-wa-way? I'll be there in an hour. O-k-k-kay, b-but the la-la-landslide happened at f-f-five. T-t-taake meee o-ooo-ver. Br-bring meee a-a b-b-boat. He'd lower the receiver from his ear, hang up and fetch his peacoat; pull on his boots and hurry down to the quay. It was impossible to rest or keep a hold on his thoughts when the crows took flight, shrieking and resettling on the lines at all hours. He used to shake his fist at them, shouting that they could damn well shut up. One morning last week he had woken to find a crow standing in his bedroom. It must have got in through the window as he slept. It studied Nils with its brownish-black eyes. O-k-k-kay, n-n-nothing to d-d-o buuuut g-g-go, e-e-eh? the crow said. Now he knows that without the crows, he would have been a poor man. Or rather, without the crows, he would have been an even poorer man. Br-br-briiing mee a-a-a b-b-boat.

In the avalanche-ridden winter of 1973, they had called from morning to night. His boat shuttled back and forth. It moved in circles, it moved in triangles and rectangles. His boat was the exception. The cars stood still, they were small and useless – all roads were suddenly cut off. Buses were stuck fast, they were heavy and bulky, able to move neither forwards nor backwards. Helicopters and seaplanes floated above the fjord, but had problems landing. His boat was in motion day and night. People put their lives in his hands. He ferried people out of chaos and into safety.

The biggest landslide happened on 11 January, somewhere between Husa and Hiller. Nils Vik had sailed over there as soon as he'd received the phone call early that morning. On board with him was the district sheriff, along with three other men. The wind was still howling and singing. Later, on the news, they said there must have been at least 150,000 tonnes of hard-packed snow in that single avalanche alone. A guy on the east side had filmed how the snow had come tumbling down and jostled two houses and a barn all the way out onto the fjord, where the buildings had remained, floating. The recording shows cars slamming on their brakes and reversing at speed to avoid being caught in the avalanche. Spruce forests and fruit trees torn up at the roots – it's impossible for them to withstand such forces – and churned over with all the debris, everything coming down, two of the houses rolling around like pieces in a game of Monopoly. After seeing this on the television Nils wrote in the logbook: *All that snow, like watching a white wig come slipping down the mountainside.*

The amateur film footage was replayed over and over, until even channels in the United States had broadcast it. Nils had seen the story a couple of evenings later, when the storm had passed and the news was now that this winter of avalanches in Norway had become news overseas. The American presenter, in a dramatic voice, had said: *This is one of the most beautiful areas in the world, but also one of the most dangerous.* Nils could have told them that. You had to learn to live with the mountains, to recognise when they're calm and when they're starting to slip and slide and creak and groan. He's stared up at those mountains for so many years. Mountains that can vanish into the fog for days before suddenly reappearing. Mountains that change slowly as you sail across the fjord, but which are always worth keeping half an eye on. Mountains that shoot up from the water, to be framed by the virgin snow and glaciers high above. Mountains with their own rules that must simply be respected, with their cracks and crevices, their chasms and voids and murderous intentions.

He'd known it long before it happened – that the avalanche would come, that there would be crashing and clanging and hammering somewhere along the fjord. The birds know these things, the animals know it, as do the fish – they know it long before humans do, they know when changes in the weather and storms are coming, they know when it will start to rain, when thunder and lightning are on the way. They have gathered this knowledge over millions of years by watching the clouds and listening to the earth; they perceive microscopic variations in the water, the ground and the air. And aboard a boat, too, it's possible to see the weather from a distance, there's no need to listen to the forecast or read the newspaper. All you have to do is notice how the fjord begins to flatten, or how the air thickens, or how the birds are moving against the sky.

That morning, they had docked at Husa and gone ashore. A couple of cows stood out on the fjord on a sheet of ice, utterly casually, as if they were sauntering around a meadow on a summer's day. How in the hell did they get out there? the district sheriff asked. Up the mountainside, one of the houses that had been caught in the avalanche appeared to be teetering on the rocky slope. The building itself had been liberated from its foundations – it was now sitting at a perilous angle beneath the heavy clouds, ready to tip over at any moment. It's about to go over, Nils had whispered to himself as they walked ashore and struggled through all the snow, it's about to go over, it's about to go over. When you see a house at night, it seems to shelter and safeguard its sleeping inhabitants – the house keeps watch and protects against danger. But this house had been reduced to a skeleton, and as they moved closer, Nils saw that one of its shorter sides was gone – it was as if a meteorite or rocket had hit the north wall and torn a great hole in it. It was now possible to see the interior, like looking into a doll's house, or a model at 1:1 scale. The elderly couple who lived there, Olina and Malvin Toft, were still sitting in the bedroom. They came into view when Nils came level with the house. The white double bed must have slid sideways, down towards one wall. There the old couple sat, with blankets and duvets piled over them so as not to freeze to death. Stay still, Nils had shouted that morning. Just stay completely, absolutely still. In reply, a thin cry came from the woman in the house. Ge-e-et u-u-uuuss o-oooouuut.

THE BOAT MOVES DARKLY THROUGH calm waters, past Dalane, Rostøy and Storoksen, everything smells of diesel and seawater and rusted iron. Nils's gaze is fixed on the dials, his hands rest on the valves and levers. Now and then he pinches his own arm to see if he's still alive. Yes, he's still living. He is still in this world. He's coming with his boat, he who was here first, he who was here before any of this, before the islands, the islets, the rock. Before the water, before the salt in the sea.

The day is finally here. The light has changed. Jon has taken a seat in the cabin, he smokes as he tunes his guitar. Luna dozes a little. On the radio, people are calling in to request their favourite songs. It's eleven o'clock – how can it be *eleven o'clock*? He's been on the fjord for over three hours already, he should have made it much further out. But the church comes into view on the starboard side, the peals of its bells trembling on the water's surface. The service is about to begin, although Nils can't see anyone outside in the churchyard.

You do know where we're going? Luna asks.

Of course I do, he says.

You're sure?

Yup.

Only, he isn't sure. He knows this stretch of the journey, but about the rest, he knows as little as everyone else. All he knows is that he has to remember. That's his assignment.

He has to remember. And he remembers, make no mistake. He remembers.

It was, by the way, the old priest who had actually been his first passenger. Back then Nils was only fourteen and didn't have his own boat, so he wasn't even the one getting paid for the trip. And you are? the priest had asked when Nils arrived to collect him. Nils Vik, he replied. And have I had the pleasure of being taken across the fjord by you before? the priest asked. No, you haven't, Nils replied. He explained that his father was indisposed, and that he was therefore standing in as the ferryman.

What had at first seemed like an easy voyage – to get the priest over to the two other churches in the rural munic-ipality so he could deliver his Sunday sermons, and then bring him safely home again – had turned into something more challenging when the wind began to pick up before the return journey. It won't be a problem if we leave right away, Nils said. The priest was vast as a county, and not especially tall in stature, but still he seemed to study Nils from an enormous height. Can you swim? the priest asked. No, I'm afraid I can't, Nils replied. Do you believe in God? the priest asked. No, I'm afraid I don't, Nils replied. Do you have a cigarette? the priest asked. No, I'm afraid not, Nils replied.

He could tell the priest was nervous. On the trip over he'd sat very still, deep in concentration in the cabin, having spread out his handwritten notes for his sermons in front of him. Now he jabbered away, quoting from the Bible, asking how old Nils was, asking whether Nils intended to make a life for himself on the sea. I don't know, Nils said, starting the motor, preparing for the journey. Give me the name of a happy seaman, the priest said. There's no such thing as a happy seaman, it's beyond the bounds of possibility.

The priest declared that if Nils took care of what was below them, he'd take care of what was above, although he believed a person could never be completely safe – especially not from himself. I'll just have to have faith that God's angels have sent you, the priest said. Nils said as little as possible – he was afraid of being asked any more questions about faith and doubt. At fourteen he was already a fully fledged ferryman, it was how he had grown up. He'd learned to read the water and the wind, the clouds and the sky; he knew how the waves would break, he knew all there was to know about bearings and rainfall and motors and makes. And with this knowledge came that other knowledge, experience gleaned by men at sea over thousands of years. Don't eat eggs before going aboard a boat. Don't whistle into the wind. Don't sing into the wind. Don't go out on Thursdays. Nor on the second Monday in August or on the last day of the year. Get a tattoo of a pig or a rooster or a swallow – these are the animals and birds that know the way home. Should you meet a red-haired woman on your way to the quay, stay ashore.

Nils angled the boat towards the wind. He would study his father whenever they were out on the fjord together – he noticed how he might joke around and laugh on a calm day, the way he would gesticulate and smile when they were docked at the quay. But the rougher the sea, the more serious his father became. He turned into a silent, austere man who tried to maintain the balance and follow the water, to make headway using the wind and waves and motor. This was the Sunday Nils himself became such a man. Nils felt the pounding of his heart, the mix of eagerness and nerves, a feeling of being older than he actually was – all the things there's no time to reflect on when standing at the wheel in foul weather. He had an important man he needed to ferry across the fjord, a big man in every sense, a man he couldn't lose.

WHO WAS NILS VIK'S MOST famous passenger? The prime minister, of course, with the cabinet minister a close second. But the only passenger Nils used to brag about having had aboard was the actor Edward G. Robinson. This was in April 1969. The film company had hired Nils to ferry people to the filming of *Song of Norway*, and that day he had taken the American and some of the cast and crew down the fjord. In the logbook, Nils has written: *Tried to explain to Robinson that he's been on board before, only in the form of reels of film, because I've been ferrying the local projectionist around for years, but my English wasn't good enough.* He had seen Edward G. Robinson in several movies – he liked *Key Largo* in particular, it was one of the few films that had stuck with him, perhaps because he himself was a ferryman and therefore recognised the environment and archetypes, but it had an exciting storyline, too. Sometimes Nils would end up going ashore to watch a film to pass the time – he had to wait for the projectionist regardless, before they could move on to the location of the next showing. *Song of Norway* he saw only a quarter of – he'd been so desperate for a smoke that he'd gone down to the boat to fetch the pack of cigarettes he'd left behind. Then he couldn't be bothered to go back. It had been his landscape up there on the screen, but it had appeared unrecognisable to him. In the logbook, he wrote of Robinson: *A pleasant acquaintance.* The actor had waxed lyrical about the fjord landscape as he stood out on the deck. What kind of a mood is this landscape in? the American had asked. A member of the crew wondered whether he believed places have feelings. They do, Edward G. Robinson said. Absolutely. Places and landscapes have genders, too. This one is clearly a man.

Which passenger does Nils wish he had never taken aboard? Trygve Stemland? Oh yes, there's one for you. Trygve Stemland – the name still makes the hairs on the back of his arms stand on end. Nils had picked up Trygve Stemland in the city on a summer's day in 1961. Stemland was taking a weekend fishing trip to Marøya, only Nils had noticed the man didn't have any fishing gear with him; he had a tent and a rucksack, but no rod, for example. Nor on the return journey had there been any talk of fish, even though Stemland had talked incessantly in a strange, mechanical voice. Even when he spoke warmly of a footballer he'd seen in action up in the stadium – a local boy who dribbled like a little magician – his voice was flat and toneless. Nils thought the man probably needed to get the city out of his system, to get some fresh air. He seemed pale and sickly, with his beard and his swept-back hair and his scar on his forehead.

The following week, Trygve Stemland had called and said he needed to make the trip out to Marøya again. That Friday Stemland was wearing a police uniform. He also had a colleague with him, a young milksop, also in uniform. Stemland informed Nils that he hadn't been completely honest the previous week, but he'd only been at liberty to share limited information regarding the action they were about to take. The case involved several complaints the police had received about the Mikkelsen family's dogs – the mangy mutts were practically taking over the island. Stemland had spent the previous weekend making observations, and ascertained with his own eyes that the dogs posed a danger to both the public and themselves; the dogs were emaciated and starving, apparently mistreated and neglected. Nils protested – he had never had a problem with the dogs there, and he often went out to the island. As far as he knew, the Mikkelsen family loved their dogs.

Have you spoken to the family? Nils asked.

No, it was the neighbours who notified us, Trygve Stemland said.

But there aren't any neighbours for miles around, Nils said.

During the journey the two policemen had spoken about how the dogs should be killed. How they could do away with them, finish them off, preferably with a single shot. Don't hesitate, don't wait, just shoot. Now that such an operation had been decided upon, it had to be undertaken properly – efficiently and humanely. Trygve Stemland said he'd learned a lot during the war. He knew how to stay cool-headed and focused for hours at a time.

It always feels good to kill someone you really want to kill, Stemland said. There, I got the bastard – like, thank God it wasn't me that hit the ground, it was *him*, nothing more to worry about, just go calmly on your way.

While the two policemen sat out on the deck in the sun, Nils checked the bags they had brought into the wheelhouse. He quickly unzipped them and peered inside. Two Winchester rifles and a lot of ammunition. He wondered whether it would be possible to get out onto the deck and throw the rifles overboard before they could stop him.

I'd be careful with that, if I were you, Trygve Stemland said. He stood there in the doorway – he had caught Nils red-handed. I've seen the damage one of those bullets can do, he said. It's quite the sight, the way a face can be blown out the back of a head.

Two hours later, dead dogs lay all over the island. At first, Nils had sat in the boat with his palms clamped over his ears, but it was impossible to shut out the salvos of shots. There were long periods of silence, then another salvo would ring out; there would be howling, then silence again. When Nils heard a wail from one of the Mikkelsen kids – a long and ghastly NOOOO! – he jumped ashore and walked up the path to the house.

He could see dead dogs in the yard and over in the field, dogs that had been flung outwards, as if by an explosion. The bodies were hacked up; entrails had poured out onto the gravel. Organs lay in the grass: livers, hearts, lungs. Contorted muzzles lay covered in dirt and a fine layer of dust. The Mikkelsen kids came running across the meadow and disappeared into the pine forest on the east side of the property. They were both screaming, and neither of them noticed Nils. The policemen were nowhere to be seen, but he could hear scattered shots from what must have been a little further north on the island. Nils went into the house. In the hallway, too, lay a dead dog. The labrador's brain matter was spattered across the floor and up the walls.

Hello? Nils called.

He received no answer.

Over in the barn, up in the hayloft in the half-dark, he found Mrs Mikkelsen. She sat huddled in a corner, a puppy clutched to her chest. Mrs Mikkelsen lifted a finger to her lips. Nils went over to her and whispered that he could take the puppy with him, down to his boat. He reached out his arms to take it. Reluctantly, the woman handed over the tiny creature. The dog trembled in his hands, whimpering and trying to wriggle free. Nils hushed the puppy as he held her nice and tight. Her name is Luna, Mrs Mikkelsen whispered. There, there, Luna, Nils soothed the dog as he ran as fast as he could over the meadow, across the yard, down the path, down to his boat. In the wheelhouse, Nils settled the tiny dog on the seat beside him and put out from the shore.

WHAT WILL YOU DO WHEN you meet Marta again? Luna asks. Why, is there something I'm supposed to do? Nils replies. The dog asks if he's being serious. *Really? Nothing?* Doesn't he miss Marta? Doesn't he think about Marta? What has he written in the logbooks about Marta? Luna wants to hear about Marta. She's heard it all a thousand times before, but just one more time, please, pretty please.

He remembers everything. Everything. No, not everything – nobody remembers everything. But Nils does remember what he thought when he saw Marta for the first time. Now here's someone who would be good for me, he'd thought. He'd been standing with his back to the bonfire, grinning in the flickering light. I know who you are, she said. You do? he replied. Of course – you're the ferryman, she said. But I don't know who *you* are, he said. Well then I suppose you're just going to have to find out, she said.

He had noticed the way she tucked her hair behind her ear – he'd loved that tiny movement, her hand lifting to her face to tuck her hair behind her ear. Will we see each other again? he had asked that first evening. No, she'd replied. Why not? he wanted to know. I just don't think so, she'd said. I understand, had been his reply.

But he didn't understand. She had extricated herself and moved on to dance with one of the city boys, one of the young men Nils himself had ferried over to the Midsummer's Day party. She had flown straight out of his arms, with her short hair, her red dress. Marta and the city boy had danced past him, right to the edge of the forest, and then they'd disappeared between the trees. After that night, he tried to find her. Just a few days earlier she hadn't existed, then suddenly she was everywhere and nowhere. He looked for her as he ferried people back and forth, he glanced about him as he delivered post and newspapers. All he knew was that her name was Marta and that she lived somewhere on the other side of the fjord, probably down in Nordrepollen. He had no idea how to go about finding her. *This is beyond ridiculous*, he wrote in the logbook. *We're separated by nothing more than a strip of deep salt water I can easily cross.* One day he docked the boat at the quay over on the other side and walked towards the house he thought must be the right one. He took the steps in two or three bounds, but then his courage failed him. He stood very still, thinking that his life was in that house, on the other side of that door, the life that was now named Marta.

One August evening in 1950, she had come cycling along. He had watched her from the window, knowing immediately that the cyclist on the gravel road below was her. She disappeared behind the rocks – and then nothing. He waited. Had she turned around and cycled away without him noticing? Should he put on his shoes and run down there? Then he caught sight of her again. Now she was pushing her bike slowly towards the garden; a moment later, there was a knock at the door. He took the time to oil his hair and comb it just so before he opened the door. She said hello, and asked if he could help her with her rear tyre. She'd got a puncture further up the road, and everyone in the village said that Nils Vik was the man to see about fixing such things.

He took her bicycle down into the cellar. It was a green Svithun, with a skirt guard on the back wheel. Nils took out his tools, while she sat on a stool and watched him work.

How did you get across the fjord? he asked.

I cycled, she replied.

You cycled over the fjord?

Yes.

And how are you planning on getting back?

I guess I'll just cycle back over again.

In the garden, Marta swung herself onto the bike's seat to test the tyre. He'd had a pump lying around in the cellar, luckily enough. Want to hop on the back and come for a ride? she shouted, braking to a stop in front of him. The job's done, Nils said. He gave her a lift home that August evening, her bike standing out on the boat's deck. She said there were rumours he'd been asking after her. That didn't mean anything, he said. She said she'd seen him standing on the front steps of her house. That didn't mean he cared, he said. She said she couldn't imagine what other errand he might have had there. He replied that he had all sorts of errands along the fjord.

It's such a shame, she said, when they had crossed the water.

What? he asked.

I think it would have been really nice, she said.

What would have been really nice?

48

What you've been wanting us to do this whole time.

Less than a year later, he proposed; less than a year later, she said yes. For the rest of their life together, she denied that she herself had stuck a hole in the rear tyre of her bike that night.

After Marta's funeral, Nils had moved onto the boat. The house had been full of people for a week, and then they all went home. Everyone returned to their own lives, as did his daughters. They had asked whether they ought to stay a little longer, but he told them he didn't want to take up any more of their time. With the house empty of people a chill had spread through the rooms and deep into his body. Now that it was no longer possible to snuggle close to Marta in the bed, the lack of warmth was all-consuming. After Marta, there was nobody who shouted down to him on cold evenings: I'm waiting for you, Nils, come and warm me up! After Marta, he would sometimes roll over onto her side of the bed, just to see if she was lying there. After Marta, he still flicked off the lamp on the nightstand and said: *Goodnight, sweetheart, sleep well*. After Marta, he whispered the words from his side of the bed, but from the other there was no longer any reply.

Life after Marta. He sat on the boat with a dram, he smoked packet after packet of cigarettes. Every morning, he retched and threw up into a bucket; he wiped sweat from his face with a cold, damp cloth. Every night he crept into the bunk in the boat's cabin, trembling, shivering. One day he was woken by a neighbour, Mrs Kråkevik, who had asked if he was managing okay. Had he been able to eat something? Was there anything she could do to help? He thinks he gave Mrs Kråkevik a bit of an earful, he can't remember exactly, but he had at least subsequently apologised for his behaviour. He'd just wanted to be alone on his boat. Still, early one morning he walked up to the empty house. He didn't turn on the lights – he thought that would only amplify the absence. At least the house was now filled with darkness. When the daylight came he shaved off his beard, cutting away most of it with scissors before he spread the foam across his face and shaved the skin completely smooth.

He walked through the rooms, gathering up the flowers from the funeral and throwing them in the rubbish. Then he went into the bedroom. From Marta's nightstand he picked up the notebooks she had written in after she lost her ability to speak. He ripped out a couple of pages, put them in the drawer of his own bedside table, and then set the rest aside to burn on the fire. He read a little of the library book Marta had been halfway through when she died: *The Summer Before the Dark*. Marta finished every book she started, even the ones she disliked. Reading is my private life, she would say. Her few pieces of jewellery he collected in a little box that he put on a shelf in the living room, for the girls to go through later. He opened the wardrobe, looked at the dresses and blouses and trousers and underwear. He could smell Marta's scent even without having to bring the clothes all the way up to his face.

Shall I suck you off? Marta had asked, that very first time they had slept together. She said it in a low voice, so calmly, as if it were the most natural and logical thing in the world to ask another person. Maybe that's why he still remembers it – to say something so directly, so beautifully and with such genuineness. Here was a person who wasn't afraid to be desired, or to express her own desire. Afterwards she had looked at him: now it's your turn, Nils. He can remember no point in his life when he hasn't loved her, or when he's doubted that she truly loved him back. Sometimes, when he turned on the radio at home and heard people harping on about being unhappy in love, all the bitter experiences of their lives, he would walk into whichever room Marta was in and just look at her. What are you staring at, Nils Vik? she might ask him then. I'm staring at you, Marta Haugen Vik. Well, you can bloody well stop it – go on, get away with you, Nils Vik.

When it came to clearing out her things, he ought to have made a plan. He'd known it would be a kind of excavation, a slow uncovering of life and time, a procedure that all spouses who are left behind must undergo. He knew that, ultimately, all that would remain was the fact that Marta was gone, but the very last item of clothing he took out was her black wedding dress. He'd started hacking and spluttering then. In the end, he felt so weak and nauseous that he threw up on the bed. Marta had wanted that dress so badly. She had seen it in a shop window one April day, when they had taken a trip to the city.

But shouldn't it be a *white* dress? he had asked.

I love this one, was her reply.

HOW MANY COUPLES HAS NILS VIK ferried over the fjord on their big day? A fair number, actually. Astrid Nes, who married Peder Utvær one day in June 1958 – *a day with patches of sunshine*, he's written in the logbook. They had bought a farm in Bjotveit, moved there and had three kids – the youngest apparently became a drummer, Nils read about him in the paper, the boy had moved to New York and become a big star over there. He ferried Kirsti Reisæter and Jan Vivelid – they got married around Christmas 1961. They had actually wanted to get married in the church in Vika, but the old priest had refused because he believed they had *lain together prematurely*, so Nils ferried them down to the registry office, and yes, you could clearly see the bump beneath the bride's white dress, no doubt about it. Who else? Johanna Jakobsdotter and Halldor Vikne – the groom had a nasty scar on one side of his face that extended a fair way down his neck, it was from back when Halldor was a boy and accidentally got boiling water poured over him; nobody along the fjord had thought Halldor would ever get married, but he did. His wife said she didn't care about the burn. The wound was not her husband.

Margit Espe and Knut Havre, they got married in 1968. Havre shot himself with an AG-3 a few years later. They had two boys and a girl. Any more? Yes, Anne Røyrane and Sveinung Gravjord, married in July 1957 – Nils has written in the logbook: *Suit each other, yes, almost like two peas in a pod.*

More still? Yes, Sigrid Espeland and Ingeleiv Lote. She was a seamstress, he a musician, they were a special couple, they ended up in Denmark, and beyond that he doesn't actually know anything more about them.

He ferried Brita Skjeldås, who married Ole Opedal – that happened on 21 July 1969, he still remembers it because that was the day the Americans landed on the moon. He had ferried the wedding procession over the fjord, from Kvitno to the church and back again, as the Americans landed on the moon.

His own wedding suit still hung, quiet and patient, in the wardrobe at home. The dark-blue suit was to be his first and last, a finely cut cotton suit, a suit that had never crumbled or deteriorated the way ordinary garments did. Nils used to take the suit from the wardrobe on special occasions, on the days that weren't like other days. He had considered putting on the suit early this morning, but then dismissed the idea out of hand. He didn't want to spend his very last day in fancy clothes.

One April day in 1951, he had dressed in front of the mirror. He had slicked down his hair with just the right amount of pomade, then inserted a flower into the buttonhole of his lapel – a daffodil, if he remembers correctly. They had walked down to the boat and chugged their way over to the registry office. Marta had chosen her sister as her maid of honour; he'd chosen his brother as his best man. They had said yes to staying together through good times and bad, and then they had kissed and sailed home again in the drizzle. At midnight he had taken off the suit and hung it neatly in the wardrobe before creeping into the bed to his wife. He had lifted her arms, pulled the black wedding dress over her head. He had felt her body against his own. Their mouths had met. He had caressed her neck, her back, her bottom; she'd guided his hand between her legs. My husband, she had said.

His only extravagance in the way of clothes was his tweed overcoat. Marta had fallen head over heels for it when they had taken a trip to the city one cold day in December – she'd thought he looked like a film star in that coat. She was the one who used to buy his socks and shirts – Nils would receive them as gifts at Christmas and on birthdays. Out on the fjord he usually stood as he's standing now, in his peacoat and a pair of good trousers, preferably in dark grey or brown, a high-necked wool sweater, rubber boots and oilskins if the weather was bad – and thank God for his long johns, a lifesaver on cold days. He's always worn long johns, even back in the days when only women wore such things.

He's always thought: as long as my clothes suit the weather, I'll survive. There were days when the wind inflated the legs of his trousers and he felt the cold in every one of the two hundred and six bones in his body. There were days he ended up standing there in the same clothes for far too long – he couldn't get ashore, he couldn't change, there were more important things than being clean and sweet-smelling. He warned his passengers, told them they ought to keep their distance, his underwear was so dirty there was a risk his balls might rot off. He'd just been happy he wasn't an older gentleman with a prostate problem – it was impossible to empty your bladder with the boat rocking and rolling like that, and it's no laughing matter, by the way, the prostate, knock on wood.

AT SELJA HE LOOKS FOR Jens Hauge – Nils had been sure Jens would be standing there, ready beside the boathouse. He glances at his watch, peers out again. The house lies half hidden on a ledge above the fjord, below the black forest. No Jens. How many years is it since that day in April when he first picked him up? Can it have been in 1966? 1967? No, 1966. A rainy day, in any event. Enough rain for an umbrella. More than enough rain for a man decked out in all his finery – good-quality suit, best shirt, pocket watch in his waistcoat pocket. Trousers pulled up just a little too high, and a flat cap covering his thinning hair.

That Saturday, Jens Hauge had responded in monosyllables all the way down to the city. Yes. No. Sure. Yes. Fine.

Well, you certainly look good, said Nils Vik.

Thanks, said Jens Hauge.

All Nils managed to get out of his passenger was that he had an important errand in the city. That was it. An important errand in the city. When Jens Hauge returned, he looked as red and febrile as the beard that covered half his face. On the way home, Nils asked the man if he wanted to tell him what had happened. Jens Hauge said he did not. He stared straight ahead, breathing deeply as if to regain his composure. The next Saturday, it had been the same story. Jens Hauge called and asked if Nils was available to make another trip to the city. Again, the rain.

Again, the umbrella. Again, all the finery. More monosyllables. Another errand.

Have you become religious? Nils Vik asked.

No, Jens Hauge replied.

An alcoholic, then?

No.

Lost your mind, maybe?

No. No.

As they set out for the city on the third Saturday in a row, Jens Hauge took a small newspaper clipping from his wallet. He handed it to Nils, then stared at the floor. It read: *Farmer, 44, seeks company. Purpose: marriage.*

A little while later, Jens looked up again.

Don't laugh, he said.

Am I laughing? Nils asked.

No, but I can see that you want to.

True – but am I laughing?

I'm sure you're laughing *on the inside.*

Jens Hauge said he hadn't wanted to reveal the purpose of his visits to the city precisely because he feared he'd be made a laughing stock. If details of his private life got out, a great collective laugh was sure to go up along the fjord, on both the west *and* the east sides – especially over on the west, there were more than a few loose screws over there.

Can you help me? Jens Hauge asked.

You want *me* to help you?

Yes, you're happily married.

How do you know I'm happily married?

I can tell just by looking at you.

You can tell I'm happily married just by looking at me?

Yes – it's perfectly possible to see whether or not a man is happily married. I can see it a mile off. But no man with love in his life can understand how hard it is to be without it, and no happy person can truly grasp just how unhappy another might be.

Jens Hauge said that in order to live a life like his, with a few sheep and apple trees on this scrap of land on a far-too-steep hillside down beside the fjord, you had to protect yourself. The only solution, he had concluded, was to find himself a wife and have children. It was simple mathematics: one was one too few. In order to survive you had to be at least two, become a family, build yourself some fortifications.

In the logbook, Nils has written: *A curious drama is playing out in the city, every Saturday afternoon at the Vågen Café.* They agreed that Nils would sit at the neighbouring table while Jens Hauge spoke with the women he'd arranged to meet. Nils could drink coffee, eat cake, and study the candidates in secret. On the way home, he would offer guidance as to how Jens should behave, how he ought to approach the candidates who were of interest.

I don't want someone who's better than me, Jens said.

Listen, Nils said, men don't always know what's best for them.

I want someone I can smooth the hard edges off, if you get my meaning.

No, Jens, you don't.

What *do* I want then? I know I want someone I can laugh with, at the very least.

But you don't seem to do much laughing.

You don't know me. I laugh quite a lot.

I think I've yet to hear you laugh even once.

I just want someone I can laugh with.

Some of the women turned up at the agreed time; others arrived late. Some had dressed up for the occasion; others looked exhausted. Several of them seemed nervous and insecure as they sat there without removing their hat or coat, only sipping at their coffee and picking at the cake in front of them – they only made Jens even more restless and red-faced. A couple of the women practically came crashing through the doors, and Jens and Nils agreed that they seemed vulgar and not worth pursuing. Often the conversation at the table ran dry a little too quickly; everything ground to a halt and Jens would be left floundering. Now and then he ended up telling rambling stories that charmed not a single contender, talking at length about his sheep getting stuck up the mountainside, or about his father, who had died after he split his head open when he fell from a chair while changing a light bulb.

You have to *see* them, Nils said. Everyone needs to be seen – there isn't a single person on this earth who isn't longing to be discovered.

He advised Jens Hauge to take off his cap. The suggestion was met with protests and the pointing out of Jens Hauge's bald patch.

But you have to be honest, Nils said. They need to know what they're getting.

Albeit a little reluctantly, Jens Hauge followed Nils's advice. He set his flat cap neatly on the table beside him and took great pains to ask the women about themselves. He tried to find out what he and they had in common, to ascertain whether they had any experience with farming. Nils began to enjoy it, sitting by the window in the Vågen Café with a view of the fish market and the fjord, listening, stealing glances. Noting how the couple at the neighbouring table attempted to untie the knots in one another. The way they tried to get to the heart of the matter, to set their words and each other in motion.

And then it happens – yes, it happens – Jens Hauge suddenly becomes visible, there in his fine suit. He sits at the same table in the Vågen Café every Saturday, a little more confident each time, and something desirable and attractive wells up in him. Nils notices it – yes, there's something solid, something unbreakable about the man. At the next table Jens Hauge is in the process of becoming himself, a man worth taking a chance on. And one Saturday in August along comes Caitlín Keegan, a thirty-three-year-old hairdresser with Irish parents. Someone who looks Jens Hauge straight in the eye, and whose gaze he dares to return. In the logbook, Nils has written: *Self-assured, solid – a catch, if you ask me.* It's a shame, Nils had said on the way home that Saturday, that you'll soon be bald – she won't have the pleasure of cutting your hair. Jens Hauge only shook his head and stared at the decking.

Then I suppose she'll just have to make do with trimming my beard instead, he said.

They arranged for Caitlín to come out to Selja with them, to see the house and farm. Jens Hauge had scrubbed and polished; he had cut the grass twice; he had shorn the sheep; he had felled pine trees to create clearings in the forest and let more light into the house. He'd washed the windows, changed the bedding, tidied all the rooms. He'd been hoping for a glorious September day, but as they made their way to the city to collect Caitlín, the fjord was grey, the mountainsides were grey, the roads were grey. The houses, the horses, the barns, boathouses and tractors – everything grey, everything wet, everything bleak. A veritable flood of rain poured down, a barrage of nails thrown at the water's surface and at the boat.

This isn't going to work, Jens Hauge said as he sat in the wheelhouse staring out through the window. This isn't going to work. What chance do I have in weather like this? Who wants to live in a landscape entirely devoid of colour? Even *I* don't want to live here on a day like this! But Caitlín Keegan was waiting on the city quay, dripping wet and smiling. She stepped aboard, introduced herself to Nils, and hugged Jens, dazzling and eager. The two of them sat in the cabin on the return journey, fresh-faced and blushing, excited and babbling. From the boat Nils saw them disappear up to the house under Jens's umbrella.

The next morning, Nils was to go and pick up Caitlín to take her back to the city – she had an afternoon shift at the salon. He docked at the quay out at Selja at nine o'clock as agreed, excited to hear how things had gone. The morning was fine and clean – the change in the weather had come a little after midnight, and Nils had stood out on the front step at home, watching as the stars were rolled out above the mountains. It was ten past nine in the morning. Then it was a quarter past nine. Half past. Twenty-five to ten. In the end Nils jumped ashore and walked up the little gravel path to find out if he'd got the time wrong, or if there was something he'd misunderstood. Out on the step, before the front door, he stopped, hesitating before knocking. Through the open kitchen window he could hear voices. The two of them were talking in there, and for the very first time, he heard Jens Hauge laugh.

AS THEY APPROACH THE QUAY at Selja and Nils finally catches sight of him, Jens Hauge's head slowly turns. He's pale, gaunt, almost grey, as if he's decomposing. There's no doubt the man is dead, but Jens smiles as the boat docks and he steps aboard. He holds out his right hand. Nils does the same.

It's been a while, Jens says.

Indeed, says Nils. How are things?

Ah, can't complain. As you might have noticed, she's shorn me to the roots.

Jens passes a palm over his shiny pate.

How did you die?

Jens laughs, and says that he died as he lived, out on the farm.

I just keeled over with my face in the dirt, arms outstretched. I remember it so clearly, lying there and knowing I was dead – it was strange, almost like realising you're alive. A snail came creeping up my left arm, and I stared at the snail and thought: well, I did my best. I did the very best I could.

And you're sure you're coming with us?

Yes, I'm at peace. Caitlín's there now, the kids are there, they'll keep the farm going.

Jens gives Nils's hand another squeeze and says he'd like to sit and rest a little, he's tired, he's waited so long. Nils nods and sends Jens through to the cabin to join the others.

It's almost twelve o'clock. The boat continues on its way, spraying up sea foam, blazing a trail through oil sheens, plastic bottles, remnants of trees, the past. Bodies merge with bodies, voices merge with low cries. Luna looks over at Nils and asks if he had any sweethearts after Marta. Nils says he didn't.

You could have done, though. There were plenty who fancied you.

Nils protests.

But I saw them! Luna says. They laughed at everything you said!

But they weren't my *sweethearts*.

Luna says women are special, that they're beautiful as birch trees. She lies quiet for a while, panting softly, before she asks if Nils ever had another dog after her.

No, I never did.

Sure?

Of course I'm sure.

Luna turns all the way around.

You could have got yourself another dog. I wouldn't have been mad – honest! It wouldn't have been, y'know, a big deal or anything.

He should have known better. The way she was standing there, the way she was staring into space, the gust of alcohol that came from her mouth. He should have said no, he should have said he had another trip to make. All he's written in the logbook about that night in July 1961 is: *Midnight trip, light southerly breeze, temperature climbed to over*

20 *today*. He and Marta had just gone to bed when they heard a screeching on the gravel outside, a car door being slammed, a motor revving up, the vehicle's hum receding. Then there was a knock at the door. Outside stood the director general's wife – the family had a summer house further down the fjord. She could pay Nils handsomely, she said, if he would take her across the fjord right away.

He should have known better, but Marta had whispered that they needed the money. They always needed money, always this constant nagging need for money. They weren't poor – well, okay, yes, at times they were poor – they had nothing to sell, it would have been great if they'd had something to sell, fruit or wool or cider or sheep, the way other folk did. For a couple of winters he'd made boat plugs down in the cellar, but it was a lot of work for very little in return. All Nils had was this boat. People used to manage, he would say to Marta when their talk turned to the family's finances, people used to manage before everyone had to have a television and a fridge and to go away on holidays – so why shouldn't *we* manage? But this had been one of life's lessons, how hard it is to think clearly when you have no money, how difficult it is when you think about everything money *can* buy, things you might feel entitled to, or wish you had. All the things other people have – like a car, for instance, or trips abroad, perhaps.

During the crossing, the woman sat in the cabin in silence. She was wearing a simple dress, with a suit-like jacket draped over her bare shoulders. She was wearing silver shoes and carrying a black handbag. The way she smoked, seeming at once both agitated and desolate, only made her appear even more attractive. She lifted the cigarette to her mouth as if in slow motion, closing her eyes on each inhalation and then blowing out, causing the smoke to rise in spirals above her head, as if she'd made smoking into an art form.

Guess how old I am, she said as she came into the wheelhouse.

Nils hesitated. She was staring straight at him.

How old would you like me to say you are? he asked.

She laughed. A strange sound that almost wasn't a laugh at all.

Do you think I'm beautiful?

He didn't reply.

Am I the most beautiful woman you've ever met?

I don't think I'm qualified to say.

She laughed again.

What happens after you've taken me over the fjord?

I wouldn't know. I'm just a ferryman.

But what happens to *you*?

To me? I'll go back home, of course.

Was that your wife who answered the door?

He nodded.

She's pretty, the woman said, and then she moved closer to him.

The woman looked at Nils in a way he still remembers, even now. He remembers thinking that this simply wasn't done, here on the fjord – it wasn't the way of the country folk, to stare so openly at another person like that, it showed a lack of etiquette. He liked to gawp at his passengers, of course, to suss them out, but only when the other party wasn't aware of it and he could study their face and gestures and movements. This woman belonged to another world. She was a different language.

I don't give a shit about your wife, she said. And neither do you.

Oh I do, I assure you.

Do you want to touch me? she asked.

He said nothing.

Touch my breasts.

He said it was impossible, that it wasn't going to happen.

Nothing is impossible, she said. You can do as you like. Touch me.

No, he said.

Don't you want me?

No, I don't want you.

That's good. A man who doesn't want you – that's always the man you want.

She sidled up to Nils. He could smell the alcohol on her breath. They stood that way for a while, face to face. Then she turned and disappeared out onto the deck. Nils glimpsed the moonlit surface of the water, the night-blue mountains, the woman's silhouette. The boat must have been somewhere around here, where it is now, just east of Bjånesøy. He was ready to react in a split-second should he have to. Standing there at the wheel he could hear his own rapid heartbeat in his ears.

After a couple of minutes the woman came back in.

Can you kill me? she asked.

Kill you?

Yes.

She said she'd give him all the money she had on her. She didn't know how much it was, but she could count it and give him a number. She suggested he might strangle her, then throw her overboard. He could squeeze her throat until she was no longer breathing, then simply get rid of her body. No one would ever find out what had happened.

He shook his head.

No? she asked.

No, he said.

What's it like, do you think? she asked.

What's it like?

To die.

He didn't respond.

She waited a little before withdrawing to the cabin and lighting another cigarette. By the time Nils had crossed the fjord again and returned home to Marta he was trembling; his hand shook as he poured himself a dram and told her what had happened. More recently he's thought that everyone has their limit – that sooner or later everyone ends up close to that border between life and death – and nobody knows just how much pain or how many defeats they'll be able to withstand before that line appears. The thing about rich people is they think they can buy anything and everything, including their own fates. Including their very exit from this life.

The woman, by the way, forgot to pay him that night. She said nothing more until they reached the other side of the fjord. As she stepped ashore, without so much as a glance at Nils, she said: Fuck you.

WHAT HAS HE LEARNED, standing here in the wheelhouse, gazing out? From staring at islands, stubble, headlands, glaciers, smallholdings, wrecked cars in gardens, the old patchwork fields, the new housing developments, this land that rises straight up from the deep fjord. What has he learned? Ah yes, this, the lesson of every day: getting up at five-thirty in the morning, getting out on the fjord, to stand here, as he's doing now, watching a wan and decrepit November sun struggle its way through the covering of clouds, and later – should it actually manage it – see how the sun runs its tongue over the mountains, first the peaks, then the slopes in the west, and then across the entire landscape. Sunlight on the trees, sun on the rooftops, the chimneys, the birds, the water. He has learned that each and every day the light hits the fjord in a new way; the sea can be pale and greyish, or it can darken, as on a winter's day, turning black as home-brewed beer. The sun might etch itself into the landscape, making the fjord seem forged of light metal, and on August mornings the sky turns lazy and content while the sea takes on a viscous calm. On a January day the wind can whip and slash white stripes into the water's thick surface, and sometimes the sea grows irascible, spitting foam and green bile. But it never happens in the same way, the same day never comes twice. It is only on this last day that the days feel like a single long one. But every day the fjord will change, the light will change, the colours will change; murky clouds will gather, and then comes the rain in monochrome – rain on the deck, rain on the windows, rain on the roof of the wheelhouse – so much rain it's like being inside a drum. Rain that comes in showers, that seems it will never stop. But towards evening the rain may abate after all, the words may abate, the motors abate, the boats abate, and night falls over the fjord, the water's surface shuffling the lights from the houses, and then you just have to find the right outdoor light, steer by only this light, make your way up to the silent house, walk bare-foot across the floorboards, tiptoe through the rooms and take yourself to bed. Sometimes nature serves up its most monumental aspects, a wind that no house or boat is built for, that not even the landscape knows of or understands, a wind that hunts you down the fjord, that causes boats to capsize, that makes houses creak and groan, that leaves walls strewn across the hills and causes roofs to lift, the way the hair of a man with a comb-over lifts. *The weather inside me changes, too*, he has written somewhere in the logbooks. *I'm like the fjord, I swell, grow calm, swell, grow calm.* Yes, a ferryman is a constant variation, reliable and to be trusted absolutely; he comes when he says he will, he floods into the fjord and ebbs out of the fjord, just like the water that crashes and pools, that accepts and embraces all things. But always onwards, onwards, like the hands of the watch on his wrist, in the direction of those already moving at speed, making headway. Soon he will turn off the motor, and all that momentum will be lost.

SHOULDN'T MISS ALSTADSÆTER be standing over there, on Bakke? Indeed she should. Nils can just see her house, the white and grey clouds hanging pillow-like above its roof, but he can't see Ingrid Alstadsæter. She appears on so many of the logbooks' pages. On calm days she would sit in the cabin with piles of marking, groaning and exclaiming in her rasping smoker's voice. Cursing, unhurriedly and sadistically. What a bunch of fools. What a bunch of goddamned idiots. How had they got *sixty-five* from seven times eight? How could they write *intresting* and *curius* and *imideately*? Just how stupid was it possible to be? She would boil them, slowly, until they'd learned the line of kings. She'd subject them to water torture until they knew their times tables. They were so backward they'd never amount to anything in this life. Not a goddamned thing.

Ah yes, there's Miss Alstadsæter. She's standing there, just as she used to. Here she is, in her grey coat and black skirt suit. Nils prepares to dock, pulling up alongside the quay; once she's aboard he wants to hug her, but she only holds out her hand. She has that impatient look in her eye, a look Nils remembers used to both impress and irritate him.

It's okay if I smoke in here, Miss Alstadsæter says.

It isn't a question. Nils takes out his pack and offers it to her. She lights the cigarette and looks at him. They stand in silence for a while. They have all manner of things to discuss, but they don't quite seem to know where to start. Nils gets the boat back out onto the fjord again.

So how did you die? he asks.

Of dehydration, she replies.

Dehydration?

Yes – didn't you know that women who live alone shrivel up? I don't know how it is for men, but a woman gets dehydrated if she spends her life alone.

You weren't happy, then?

Happy? Only mediocre people are happy.

She glances at him.

I was well and truly wrong about you, Nils. Here you still are, buzzing about on the fjord. Just how old are you, anyway?

Nils can't help but grin, but he says nothing.

I remember how well you did at school. Did you have no ambitions?

Of course I did, but I got my first boat when I was fifteen.

What a fool – such a good head on his shoulders, and he quits school to ferry people across a fjord.

Ah, it could have been worse. I took care of people, ferried them here, there and everywhere – including *you*, in case you've forgotten.

Tell me, Nils, how could it have been worse?

Nils chuckles.

Oh, I know I was a terrible person, she says. Go on – you can just go ahead and say it.

You were a terrible person, Ingrid Alstadsæter, Nils says.

Thank you. And don't think I'm about to ask *you*.

About what?

Whether or not you were happy – because I know exactly what you'll say. You're one of those people who thinks you're happy where you are, somebody who wants no more than what you already have.

I was happy.

Did I *ask* you?

No, but I *was* happy. I just continued to do what my family had always done.

Miss Alstadsæter lets out a brief laugh. Oh, I think I probably did the same. I was depressed, just as my mother was depressed. Her mother was depressed, and her mother too – they were all depressed, I came from a goddamned depressed family. It was a family tradition I took extremely seriously – and I have to say, the capability level of the kids here in this fjord helped a great deal.

She says it had been her mission in life to provoke as many of the kids as possible into rising above themselves, in order to lift them out of the fjord. There was no future here, nothing but narrow-mindedness and stagnation. She asks Nils where he thinks an alien from another planet would go to find out how things work here on Earth. Would they come here? Here, to this fjord? No, the alien would go somewhere it's possible to study humanity's greatest achievements, like Rome or Paris or Athens. Not here. Never here.

So how come you never simply moved away? Nils asks.

She thinks for a moment before she replies.

I moved here and ended up staying, she says. But I never *lived* here.

Ingrid Alstadsæter asks if Nils can do her a favour; she wants him to go down into Brusundet. Nils looks at his watch. Twelve-thirty. He says he hadn't been planning on going that way, but it's no trouble, they can go through Brusundet. He turns the boat to starboard. He looks towards Dalemyr and Skuggestrand and sees the houses on the western bank, the white ones and the yellow. Sees the boathouses along the beach, the red ones, the grey.

I think I was hoping she'd be waiting for us, Ingrid says as they approach Brusundet.

Who? Nils asks.

She nods towards the burnt-down house on the rocks up ahead. Only the foundations remain. Kari Aga is nowhere to be seen on the quay. The wide, grey fjord, the sound, a burnt-down house. No Kari.

She was the reason I moved here, Ingrid Alstadsæter says.

Kari?

Yes, yes, Kari, of course.

Nils has to collect himself.

I didn't know that, he says. What happened?

Nothing, she replies. That's precisely what happened. Nothing.

She glances at Nils and says that in the very first year after she'd moved here, so the two of them could at least be geographically close to one another, Kari Aga had married. And then she'd had three children, one straight after the other. Three kids in three years – Ingrid's beloved had suddenly been transformed into a birthing machine.

But I can't really blame her for it, either, Ingrid Alstad-sæter says. It wouldn't have been an easy life. Not here, not with me.

Nils should have realised – and he's always thought of himself as such a good judge of character. He'd lost touch with Ingrid Alstadsæter after the district schools were closed down. Then he'd begun ferrying the students to the teacher, rather than the teacher to the students. But one autumn evening around ten or twelve years ago, Ingrid Alstadsæter had called to ask if Nils would be travelling by boat to Kari Aga's funeral. She said that funerals were vile, loathsome things. She needed someone to accompany her, and besides, her sight wasn't what it used to be, these days she simply refused to drive in the autumn darkness. But she would like to attend the funeral, she had many good memories of those trips down the fjord with Kari and Nils.

Kari Aga's funeral had taken place in the pouring rain. A rain that soaked the church and the trees and the earth, a rain that drenched the stoop-shouldered country folk, all dressed in black beneath their umbrellas, all unmoving and speechless, these people who had come to see the local midwife to her final resting place. Several of them must have been brought into the world by Kari, or else they had children or grandchildren who had been welcomed by her. Nils saw the napes of necks, the backs of heads, the coffin that was borne out, with three men on each side and Kari Aga's sons walking behind, out through the doors, out into the rain, out to the hole in the ground.

On the return voyage after the funeral, Ingrid Alstad-sæter had stood with Nils in the wheelhouse, just as she's doing now. She had chain-smoked and said little. Usually she prattled away, but that day she'd hardly said a word. Yes, he really should have realised.

Ingrid stubs out her cigarette against the wall and flicks the butt out of the side window.

You know how it is, don't you? she asks.

No, how is it?

You know, when you walk into a room and see a face, and then you realise you belong to that person, forever.

She snaps her fingers.

Just like that, she says.

Just like that? he asks.

Ingrid Alstadsæter tells him about the night she had cycled out to Brusundet. It was the first week after she'd moved here, back when she still believed they would be together, she and Kari. That night, she had walked up to the front door of the house and noticed how the lights were on inside. As she stood on the front step and fixed her hair and straightened her coat, she knew that in those illuminated rooms was a woman, not entirely unlike herself, who would soon hear the knock – who would walk down the stairs, cross the hallway, move to open the door – and she had stood there on that August evening, trembling and ready, filled with a time that was meant to be without end.

YES, HE SHOULD HAVE REALISED. It's obvious, now that he thinks about it. Kari Aga, always waiting there on the quay, always punctual, always in her dark coat with the collar turned up against the wind and the cold, her black bag clutched in her hand. Nils would go into Brusundet to pick her up, always with a flask of coffee, and they would chit-chat while Kari perused the newspaper or stared out of the windows. They talked about the weather, fishing, family life. He no longer remembers how it had come to pass, but they'd created a kind of ritual they performed after each birth – they would share a cigarette and a small glass of cognac to celebrate the fact that a new life had come into the world. Nils had learned a lot from Kari – he didn't attend the births, of course, but he sometimes had to assist in the event of complications, and he'd made a habit of listening when the midwife told him about the various deliveries. One March morning in 1975, a baby girl had announced herself too early, as Nils was ferrying her pregnant mother to a check-up. The tiny thing had arrived like a shot and lay there, unmoving, on the floor of the cabin. Blue. Still. Not breathing.

There was complete silence in the cabin. It had become the kind of space in which sound did not exist. Nils knew he had to hold the baby upside down, massage her, gently slap her cheeks. After what seemed like an entire hour, an entire day, an entire lifetime, the baby girl began to hiccup. She coughed, she spluttered, and then Nils heard the girl's voice. She wanted to live. She was going to live. Her whining filled the cabin, the sound fine and thin as a silken thread through the air. Nils, too, had been holding his breath – he had automatically put his own breath on hold, for how long he didn't know, but now he stormed out onto the deck. The boat had drifted into the middle of the fjord, a flock of seabirds had gathered above it, and Nils drew the air deep into his lungs and shouted *Yeeeeees!* Sometimes, it's a beautiful world. And seventeen or eighteen years later Nils ferried a young woman, friendly and smiling, dark-haired and long-limbed, a woman who, after she had stepped aboard in Vika one summer's day, stuck her head into the wheelhouse. She said her family had moved away from the area when she was a couple of years old. Did Nils remember her? Did Nils remember that morning, when she had come into the world, right here?

What other births? He remembers Tora Heggøy – nobody had thought Margit at the local store would ever be a mother, she must have been over forty when she took up with Guttorm Langnes, a skirt-chaser who drank and went on many a bender and who wasn't a particularly good farmer, or a particularly good father for that matter – he vanished from the lives of mother and daughter shortly after the birth. But Margit had the child she'd been dreaming of her entire life, a lovely daughter who stood behind the counter beside her mother from when she was just a little girl. He remembers Lars Fasting, who was born under the open sky in 1971, early one morning on the county road at Tveitane. A huge pine had fallen across the road, and the parents-to-be were unable to get to the hospital. The father had run to the nearest neighbour's house and called Nils. Br-iiing me a boooaat. He remembers the blue morning and the tiny boy Kari pulled from the mother, with such force that the child almost sang; goats and sheep had gathered, the animals stood gawking in the mist as the baby opened his mouth and mewled.

He remembers Sjur Mjøs, born with a club foot – the midwife had made the parents aware that the boy had a club foot, but they were just so glad to have him, he meant so much to them, and later in life the boy with the club foot became a national basketball champion playing for Gimle in the city. Sjur Mjøs grew up to be of fairly average height, but he had this incredible ability to throw a ball into a basket, over and over again. Eli and Guro, of course. At both births Nils had stood outside the bedroom door at home, waiting, hopping from foot to foot, going down to the cellar, reading the newspaper without absorbing a word. Then he was finally allowed in, and he stood over the bed with his heart full of the newborn, even though this was long before he would know who she was. He remembers Eli – she had almost managed to crawl her way to the breast unaided, that's how strong Eli was. She had sought the nipple, eager as a piglet. She opened her eyes, latched on, and in that moment it seemed her eyelids fluttered and her little eyes rolled back in her head.

*

Late in the autumn of 1983, Kari Aga called and asked Nils to come and see her at home in Brusundet. He asked what it was about, but she said only that she'd appreciate it if he made the trip. She was waiting at the kitchen table with coffee and a bar of chocolate. She said she'd get straight to the point. She took out a shopping list, which she gave to Nils. If he would be so kind as to procure the goods on the list and transport them to Brusundet every Monday, it would be a great help. He could put the items down in the boathouse, and she would leave the money for him in an envelope. Nils glanced at the shopping list in Kari's handwriting:

Butter
Bread
Potatoes
Herring fishcakes
Pork loin
Salt
Cheese
Flour
Milk
Stuffed cabbage leaves
Coffee
Freia milk chocolate
Sundries

Nils said it would be no problem at all – and that of course he'd be happy to bring the shopping all the way up to the house. Kari Aga said she'd appreciate it if he *didn't* come up to the house. Nils sat there without speaking. He glanced at Kari, but nor did she say anything further, and an uncomfortable feeling settled over the room.

In the end, Kari stood and sighed.

This will be my last winter, she said.

Nils paused. Said something about how he'd surely be far more useful if he brought the shopping up to the house each Monday and looked in on her. Then he added that he was very sorry to hear she was ill.

Well, you live for a time, and then it's over, Kari said.

She said she couldn't bear all the hypocrisy, all the false care and concern. She wanted to die alone, she didn't want others to see her sick and weak – that wasn't the way she wanted to be remembered. Nils was given direct orders not to say anything to anyone. She hadn't even told her own children – they had long since embarked on their own lives out east. She said that on a Monday in the near future, when Nils arrived with the shopping and discovered she hadn't collected his previous delivery, he'd know it was over.

He followed her wishes to the letter. He purchased the groceries, put everything in a crate and set the crate in the boathouse, then loyally set out from the shore again, even though each and every Monday he considered going up to the house to check in on her. Every now and then Kari would allow herself a can of good tea, or a cake. Sometimes there was a note included with the money, some brief instructions about purchasing a few special items or a new type of bread or flour.

That year, as Christmas approached, Nils had revealed the details of his assignment to Marta – she'd begun to wonder why he was buying all these groceries every Monday – which had almost resulted in a full-blown argument. Marta thought he had a duty to do more for Kari Aga. Then what should I do? he asked. Love requires that you get out and do something, she replied. He was tempted to say that that was precisely what he'd been doing, getting out there and doing her shopping, but he held his tongue. Everyone wants to die in their own way, Nils said. You can't just stand idly by and watch a person you love die alone, Marta said. She *wants* to die alone, Nils said. Nobody wants to die alone, Marta said, everyone wants to die surrounded by the people they love. He said that was the problem – Kari's husband had already passed away, and she now had only minimal contact with her children, he wasn't quite sure why, something must have gone wrong there.

But one Monday in April he had carried the crate of groceries all the way up to Kari's house after all. From out on the fjord he'd noticed the column of smoke rising up over Brusundet, and the sight of Kari crossing the yard with a stool in one hand and a glass lampshade in the other startled him – for a brief moment he thought she was already dead, that he was looking at a ghost. Kari had grown thinner over the course of the winter. Her hair was split and ragged, and as he approached he could see how her hands were white and covered with liver spots and visible veins.

Oh good Lord, she said.

Then she walked over to the bonfire that was burning on the flat coastal rock and threw the stool and the glass lampshade into the flames. She continued to fetch things from the house, all sorts of objects, which she carried across the yard and threw onto the bonfire: books and newspapers and spindle-back chairs and bedding. Nils knew neither what he should do, nor what he was now witness to.

Well, don't just stand there staring, Kari said. Make yourself useful.

Nils put down the crate of groceries and began to carry out the furniture and photographs and all manner of things that were piled up inside the house. Together they cleared the rooms, emptied wardrobes and chests of drawers, brought mattresses down the stairs. Together they worked without speaking. They emptied the conservatory, the living room, the kitchen, loft and cellar. Everything was carried outside. Tapestries, socks, tablecloths, cardigans, make-up, children's clothes, ring binders, notebooks. Nils stopped beside the grandfather clock in the hallway and said he was certain Kari could get a good price for it. She simply stared at him, then turned back to her work.

At times it seemed the fire was about to die out, that all the house's contents were not enough to feed it. Then Kari fetched a can of paraffin and poured some onto the flames, causing them to blaze up again. As they worked their way through all the objects in the house, Nils thought about just how many ways there are to bring about a fall in one's own life, how little it takes, and how unrectifiable it is, once the hole is there and you trip and start to fall. After they had emptied most of the house they stood there, staring into the flames. Everything went up in smoke. Cushions, slippers, towels, oven gloves, winter coats, blouses, underwear, pencils, paintings, trunks and chests. From behind the fire rose the evening, the shadows starting to break through.

I'm glad you came, Kari said. Do you have a cigarette?

Nils took out his pack, and they each lit up. They stood without speaking. For a moment, Kari leaned against his shoulder. He put his arms around her in a clumsy sort of way before she extricated herself, straightened her cardigan and crossed her arms over her chest. They stood there, watching how the flames wolfed down everything, this fire that ravenously moved from object to object, this fire that devoured what had once been her life.

Oh, the idiocy of having to depend on others, she said.

THE BRIDGE APPEARS ON THE HORIZON, a slim bow of steel and cement. The boat continues to glide across the fjord, it's now a quarter to two. The sun is out, a bloody egg that comes into view between stacked rain clouds, but which quickly disappears again. Then a few individual rays stream down towards the water's gleaming surface. His last sunshine. It's a fine November day, mild and magical. This mustn't end. Surely it has to endure. But it's his last day, and all along the bridge the dead have lined up, from one abutment to the other. Are they about to jump? No, they're waiting. They're simply standing there. Death awaits. Death, biding its time. The dead now come from all around, they follow the boat, the way the seagulls do. They follow Nils and whisper: Now you are one of us.

When they have passed the bridge, Nils turns and looks up. The dead have turned around and walked over to the railing on the other side. They remind him of kids watching for a model boat that's been sent down a river or out onto the fjord. Nils allows his eyes to roam and sees that these are the people he's ferried back and forth, the ones who have sat in his cabin rolling cigarettes and sipping coffee, the ones who got worked up over politicians and football matches and neighbours, who dreaded school and visits to the doctor, who looked forward to weddings and week-ends away in the city. A dead son. A dead daughter. A dead brother. A dead mother. A dead friend. Those who have passed out of their families, out of history, out of time, and away.

When the bridge was being built, Nils ferried workers and engineers from the cluster of workmen's huts to the building site, from the barge to the tower crane. He asked the crane drivers what it was like to work high in the sky and play God – he himself preferred there to be water under his feet, the waves, the fjord's surface like a floor of silver on fine days. Well, you'll just have to come up and see, was their reply. After having been teased a sufficient number of times – the crane drivers said Nils must be afraid of heights – he accompanied them over to the concrete foundations on the eastern bank, foundations that rose from the fjord and continued up into a dream.

High in the clear air he looked westwards, saw rugged rock, forests, patchwork fields, the sea beyond; to the east he saw mountains and the interior. How had he lived here for all these years without ever seeing the place like this? Not just his own tiny bay, but how things fit together, the landscape, the airspace, the distances between everything. Now he was also able to see the work up close, the way the men welded, hammered, pounded, poured concrete, tensioned cables, all while fastened to lines and ropes in order to cheat death. Nils wasn't afraid of heights, but he felt dizzy. The thought of falling, of plunging over the edge, meant that right then it seemed everything that had been, his entire life, was of a duration no longer than the time it would take to fall through the air, from the crane into the fjord below.

The night before the opening of the bridge, a joyrider had got past the cordons and driven across, headlights blazing and loud music blaring from the open windows. The police turned up, but by then the joyrider was long gone. On the day of the opening, Nils Vik's boat was full of important people – the prime minister, the secretary of state, the mayor and a number of journalists were all on board. Nils Vik had been hired so they could view the bridge from the south side. They stood out there on the deck in the sun and talked about workplaces, industry, the burgeoning road network. They spoke about this being a historic day, about the dawn of a new age. They didn't speak to him, the ferryman who would lose his livelihood to the bridge, the man who paid his bills with the money he received for ferrying around the people who lacked bridges and who therefore had to call Nils Vik. The ferryman who loves this bridge all the same. It's a marvel, a wonder, beyond all comprehension – a piece of civilisation hanging in mid-air, astonishing, with its towers and cables, its adorning necklace of lights at night. Yes, human beings built this masterpiece, human beings have thought, reflected, calculated – achieved this impossibility. Humankind seemed always to be reaching new heights. And what has *he himself* created? What chances has he taken? What visions has he had?

On the day of the opening, the photographers had viewed Nils through their lenses; the journalists had stood there with their microphones and notepads, and yet Nils didn't exist. The journalists were so slapdash, so flustered, so worked up. Nor did the landscape truly exist – presumably they saw it, and possibly they even loved it, perhaps they appreciated it that day – but they didn't see the landscape's working side, all the grey, the laboriousness, the drudgery, the struggle in every day. This unrivalled, man-made place, shaped by forgotten working folk. One of the journalists had scribbled down his name on his pad – Nils had been included in a photograph that featured the prime minister. When the image appeared in the newspaper, they had misspelled his name. He had become *Niels Wiig*.

Here – take my face. Take it, just take it. You want my face, then here it is. The face that was, the face that's no longer a part of time, the face that is passing out of time. A face that slips past, the way almost all faces slip past, those of the invisible and the faceless. Fishermen, farmers, bricklayers, housewives, teachers, charwomen, midwives, ferrymen. Those who made the villages and towns, the ones who lived there and who are now losing sight of the landscape. Some faces remain radiant, stubbornly refusing to change; others alter, surrender, get lost, or remain who they are. It is time itself that exists in them. You can see adversity in those faces, you can see joy there, so many things exist in those faces. In brief glimpses we might see who we really are, as in the early morning, just after we've woken up and turned to face each other. Some faces tell all, keep you posted, let you know when they get up and go to bed; they reveal their hopes, disclose everything they dream about, whether with eyes closed or open. Give us each day our daily face. Some faces withhold, hiding their true face. But take my face. Here is my face, it's no longer worth much, weather-beaten as the landscape, wrinkled as the water's surface. I am Nils Vik, I am a man with a boat. I crossed the fjord in a boat full of faces, there's little that can compare to it, this boat that tentatively put out in the mornings, that sidled back again in the evenings, found its way home, sailed starboard home. My face was here. Soon it will no longer exist. I'm losing speed, I'm wandering in air, I'm turning to water, this great percentage of me that is water, my face that once again will be water. *I'm waiting for you, sweetheart.*

THE OUTERMOST PART of the fjord now. Gråfjord. Svart-skjær. Krossøy. The landscape opens, clouds pile up, currents of air probe at the sea. The fjord has swollen and is now receding again; each high tide has its ebb. The afternoon has begun its journey up the mountainsides. Dusk will soon come to settle over the boat. The machinery works below him – the motor of this boat has been replaced only once, when he put in a powerful Bukh diesel engine in the mid-60s. If you can manage to keep such a motor from rusting, it'll run forever. He checks the diesel tank, sees that the needle on the gauge has gone up. What the hell? The needle has gone *up*? He taps the glass. Yes, the needle has gone up. He has more diesel now than he did when he set out. That's how it is when you're sailing back in time – the boat sorts things out, the boat knows what's best. He taps the Omega, too. Wasn't it just a quarter to two? Now the watch suddenly shows half past. This is an Omega Seamaster, it can't possibly be wrong. It feels as if time is rushing out of him. He is still in this body. Time exists in his body, time exists in his head, everyone exists somewhere between the two, between the body and the soul, between backwards and forwards, between the two halves of the puzzle, trying to make everything add up. Time begins the day you're born, and little by little you grow stronger, taller, wiser, faster, more articulate, and then comes the slow decline. You grow weaker, slower, more vulnerable, less keen to try things. He knows this now. It begins slowly, and it ends slowly. Nils Vik lifts a match to his cigarette, lighting it with slow movements. He closes his eyes, listens to the motor. Steady, steady, I have time. I have all the time in the world. He's on his way out of the fjord, he's moving in an orderly fashion and at a certain speed, he's sure of that, but in all likelihood he must have moved through a vast, circular arc.

Not too long ago, he had read in the newspaper about a theory that posited that there are not four cardinal points but only two, forwards and backwards, and that the distance between forwards and backwards is illusory – that is, a journey is a hallucination. According to this same theory, the Earth is therefore *sausage-shaped*. How he'd laughed his head off when he read that! It was an Irish philosopher who had thought up these things. Nils wakes Luna and tries to explain the theory to her. The dog is sleepy and nods sedately. She thinks for a while, then says that out on the fjord, the way is like that, there is only forwards and backwards. She also thinks the way is much more pleasant out on the water than it is on land. There the path is hard and old and creepy.

She stretches, yawns.

On land, you sort of take the place with you, Luna says. No matter how far you might run, you can never shake off the place.

What does he remember best? Ah yes – a Sunday morning when he's trying to have a lie-in, he needs sleep, all the sleep he can get, he's been out on the fjord all night. He wakes from a dream, his boat is going down, the wheelhouse slowly filling with seawater; he's at the bottom of the sea, he's underwater, lying there helpless on his back, his face turned to the surface. Then he's suddenly wide awake, one ear full of liquid, both girls sitting on top of him. Eli and Guro have brought a bottle of water into the bed; they giggle when they see his reaction. There is no happiness like this, a Sunday morning, with the early sun hanging above the mountains on the other side of the fjord, a light that settles over the bedclothes, over the floor, over his girls. He hears their breath, their laughter. They explain that they're conducting an experiment on him, they're testing whether it's possible to get water to run through his head, into his left ear and out of his right.

On the morning in August that Guro left home, Nils fried her an egg. He made her coffee and pancakes, he set out the plum jam for her, but she wasn't hungry. She only pushed the egg around her plate with her fork, taking occasional sips of her coffee.

Homesick already? Nils asked.

She stuck out her tongue at him.

Marta said goodbye to their younger daughter down on the quay, asking her to call as soon she arrived. Guro's boyfriend was there too, he didn't want to let go. They stood a little way from the boat, speaking in low voices as they hugged each other. When the two of them finally walked towards him, Nils saw that his daughter's boyfriend had been crying. Nils had almost started crying himself the night before. He'd poured himself a dram and grown sentimental.

Who would *they* be, once both girls had moved out? What kind of house would this be? Marta had teased Nils, saying his face looked like that of the neighbour when he was waiting for the truck to come and collect a dead cow. You can't say things like that, Nils complained. I'm only talking about your expression, she said, going over to him where he stood by the window, looking out. She leaned against his back and wrapped her arms around him.

As they sailed to the city that morning, Guro sat in the wheelhouse with a smile on her lips.

What are you smiling about? Nils asked.

I'm just wondering how long it will take for you or Mum to go storming into my room and tear my posters from the walls.

No, those posters are staying right where they are until you come home again.

She laughed and looked at him.

Will you write about this in your logbook?

What – you and me on a little jaunt to the city?

Yes – what will you write?

We'll see.

He sees that all the logbook entry from that day says is: *Good visibility. Fair. South-westerly.* He had known there and then that this was definitive. He could hold his daughter when they arrived, hug her the way her boyfriend had hugged her, as if to punish her, but just as Nils had fought to stay, his girls had fought to get away. He had given them all his love, all his care, but it wasn't enough. Eli had gone. Guro was now on her way.

This was how he saw it: he was a man out on the fjord, he was an explorer, but his geography was limited. He had never taken the family anywhere. Marta had dreamed of seeing Versailles – he had no idea why, but she'd seen photos of the gardens there, the lawns and hedges and flowers. He himself had dreamed of waking in foreign cities, in hotel rooms in Rome or London or New York, walking out into the sun or the rain, watching the black or yellow taxis rushing past, feeling all four seasons in the air. Of course, the girls had accompanied him aboard the boat, but it smelled of sheep shit in here. It smelled of blood, sweat, urine. He couldn't deny it, and sometimes he'd even had to ferry injured people, yes, even *dead people*; sometimes he'd had to take sheep to the butcher's, and the sheep shat themselves because they were terrified for their lives. The girls had hated that smell. He'd scrubbed and hosed everything down, but a hint of that smell would always remain. That same, shameful smell.

As they approached the city that day, it was Guro who had come over and put her arms around him.

Are you okay, Dad? she asked.

Yes, he said. Will there be someone there to meet you?

Yes, Dad, there will.

Do you have money on you?

Yes, Dad.

Got your passport?

Yes, Dad.

Umbrella?

Yes, Dad.

Contraception?
Yes, Dad.
Do you love me?
Yes, Dad.

ROBERT SOTH IS WAITING at the service station at Sund. He's standing under the neon lights in the gloaming, as if he's been standing there for years. Bomber jacket, jeans, camera around his neck, sunglasses whatever the weather. Right hand lifted, thumb high – always with his thumb out. *Hey, Mister Ferryman!* Nils had explained that the people who lived along the fjord rarely attempted to hitchhike by boat. In reply, Robert had said that it worked fine for him – just look, every time Nils came chugging along, he got a ride.

Got a smoke? Robert asks once he's stepped aboard.

Have you been waiting long? Nils asks.

Yes, and I've been smoking like you wouldn't fucking believe, smoking is the only thing a dead man can do to pass the time.

The American must have been standing there for a good long while; he stretches as he lights the cigarette, shifting his weight first to one foot, then the other. Nils sticks a cigarette in his mouth, but neglects to light it just yet. The boat drifts away from the quay. Robert has combed his hair into a side parting; it's still sharply oiled but is grey now, all of him is grey – grey clothes with grey stains, the light in the wheelhouse illuminating his grey eyelids above his small eyes. Nils had liked the American from the first day he'd met him; he hadn't hesitated to take the guy aboard when he'd suddenly appeared out of nowhere. Robert Soth explained he'd been lured here by rumours about *the dirty books of Norway*, they were said to be full of Norwegian girls in their natural state, but he hadn't seen so much as a glimpse of the books or the girls. Robert used to stay with Nils for weeks at a time, before moving on to photograph other places in Norway. Then he'd turn up again, with his camera and his smile and his right thumb stuck out: Give me a lift, let me aboard, take me along. Nils had watched him, listened to him, filled his head with Robert's stories, speech and knowledge. He had taken Robert in, guided him, helped him to find his feet, to anchor himself. Somewhere in the logbooks Nils has written: *You don't ever get two friends like this, you get only one such friend in a lifetime.*

On their trips down the fjord, Robert Soth would sit in the wheelhouse with his camera round his neck and Luna in his lap. He wanted to go into nooks and crannies, he wanted to go down lesser-known branches of the fjord – he declared, in a loud voice, that he loved the fjords. THE FUCKING FJORDS! He wanted to keep the door and side windows open. I want to hear the air and the mountains, he said, I want to hear the rocks and the clouds. We're going to freeze to death, Nils said.

Wait, wait! What's down there, Nils?

Down there? Nothing.

There must be something, *nothing* doesn't exist. Come on, let's go down there.

Robert Soth had told Nils he wanted to make memories of places nobody had ever been before. Memory was rebellion. Memory was resistance. Memory said: *We were here too!* He wanted to tell the story of Norway after the war, a country that was being rebuilt. He couldn't take any more war and death and wickedness. He'd been in Huế and Saigon during the Vietnam War, at times with an international press corps who acted as if they were on an excursion. He'd had to get away from them, he'd wandered around alone on the outskirts of Huế. The bodies of the murdered had lain in the streets and in the roadside ditches; he'd heard a girl crying out for help. Her light-coloured clothes were dark with bloodstains. She had died in his arms that afternoon, died before he could get her to a doctor or a hospital. The girl had hardly breathed her last breath when a man with a cart came past. He took the dead girl and threw her atop the cart bed, which was already piled high with bodies. Right there and then, Robert Soth had decided to spend the rest of his life photographing nothing but middle-of-the-road subjects.

Robert leans his head against Nils's shoulder. They stand that way for a while, and then Robert looks up at Nils. He has the same heavy head, and the slowest, most beautiful smile Nils has ever seen.

I thought we'd grow old together, Robert grins.

Me too, Nils says.

He extricates himself from the American.

You just disappeared.

Yeah, I just disappeared.

And then you died?

Then I died.

Nils asks what happened. Was it some disaster? Was it an accident? Had he intended to return to Norway? Robert says he travelled around back home, taking a little work here, a little there – he'd accepted a job as a stills photographer on a couple of feature films, one of them was being shot outside Alberta, Canada. While the actors stayed at a four-star hotel, he spent his nights in a filthy motel with a bastard of a dog that stood right outside his window and barked, twenty-four seven.

I woke up early one morning because my motel bed was ablaze, Robert says. I must have lit a cigarette when I was half asleep, maybe I was still a little drunk, I'd been drinking heavily the night before, an ember must have dropped from my cigarette and set fire to the comforter, the whole bed just exploded.

He laughs.

Crazy, right?

Yeah. Crazy.

As the flames rose up around him, Robert had thought about how he'd travelled across half the world, yes, all the pain and suffering he'd seen and documented, all the crises he'd survived, and now here he was, alone in a motel bed in some godforsaken town in Canada, staring up at the ceiling as he was cooked alive. What a goddamn life, huh?

Nils remembers the Sunday Robert had told him he was going back to the States. It was an unusually fine summer's day – they had chugged out to Sandøy to go swimming and drink beer and barbecue hot dogs. Marta and the girls had come along, the light had washed the entire fjord clean, the sun prickled the backs of their heads. Heat hung in the air, sluiced over their skin.

Why? Marta wanted to know.

Well, I haven't been home for a while, Robert explained. I just need to get my affairs in order, earn a little money.

A silence spread, a silence Nils knew he had to break.

So how long will you be away for, Bob? he asked.

I honestly don't know, Robert replied.

But when will you be back?

I'm not sure.

Marta had suddenly got up and begun to walk along the beach. Nils could see from the way she wrapped her arms around herself that she was upset. He'd simply thought they had both been in thrall to the American's energy, his enthusiasm, his way of being, the way he'd infiltrated their lives. There is power and potential in a friendship, something that guarantees a friend's existence and presence, even if he's moving away.

Could you lend me some money for the flight? Robert had asked.

Did you love her? Nils asks. It takes a while for Robert to answer. He's opened the left-side window. He smokes, staring out into the twilight darkness.

Marta? he says finally.

Yes. Did you love her?

Yes, I loved her.

Are you sure?

Of course I'm not sure.

Is that why you disappeared?

The American says he should have done what a man ought to do in such a situation – he should have explained, tied up the loose ends – but he'd thought that if he just went away, if he no longer saw Marta or heard her name or stared up at the same mountains she stared up at, then one fine day he might be able to breathe again.

Robert pauses. Nils waits.

Nothing happened, Nils.

Nothing happened?

No, I left before anything could happen.

You tried to destroy a family.

Did I? No – I tried to save a family. I packed up and left, and I hated having to leave, but I did it, Nils. I wanted the life you had, but I left.

Silence falls between them.

Robert asks about Marta, asks how she died.

You don't get to ask me about that. No way.

They stare at each other.

But did *you* never long for another, Nils?

Another woman, you mean?

Yes – when people long for something, they don't long for what they have, but what they *don't* have.

Oh shut your mouth, Bob.

Why should I shut my mouth? Why can't I criticise *you* for being terrible at adultery? It's unhappiness that drives people, Nils – the tragedies of life.

That's a load of piss, and you know it as well as I do.

But what's happiness good for? What about desire?

What about doubt? Jealousy? What's a life without grief and pain? You're like someone who only ever finishes the first chapter of the books they read.

Well, thanks a lot. She was my wife. Mine.

But that's what I remember best, Nils, how it is to want another person, to long for unknown skin, to imagine her, in her nightdress or naked, pushed up against the wall.

You can't talk like that about something we shared.

What did we share?

Marta. We both loved Marta.

They stand in silence for a while. Nils takes a step in Robert's direction. He puts his arms around his friend, holds him. The American releases him, says he needs to rest for a while; he wants to go into the cabin and lie down. It's hard work being dead.

Nils nods, is quiet for a time. Then he says they thought Robert had taken his own life – both he and Marta had thought that. They had received the call several weeks after his death, it was Robert's older brother who had called from Los Angeles to say Robert had been buried at home, and that was all they were told. For a long time Marta had been utterly distraught – she was sure Robert's death had been her fault.

No, no, it's just as I said, Robert says. A tiny ember. Puff. And then life was over. It was quick. Got another one? Please?

He laughs, pauses in the doorway.

Marta died of a stroke, Nils says. She survived one, but then she suffered another. And that was that.

Robert runs a hand through his hair, looks down at the decking. Then he asks how Nils found out.

I found the photographs, Nils says.

WHAT HAD THE AMERICAN PHOTOGRAPHED? He photographed fishing boats in the twilight, like illuminated eyes above the dark fjord. He photographed an old woman out in the fields, in her dress and apron. He photographed three kids coming running down the meadow, the brothers first, their little sister behind them, the white dog up beside the house – they're running towards the quay, the boat is here with their father on board, at last, at long last. He photographed men gazing out across the water, stalwart and self-assured, like extras in a film. He photographed a funeral procession. He photographed Luna, waiting outside an ice cream kiosk. He photographed Marta. She's sitting on the bed, in her underskirt and bra; she raises her hands to her hair, taking out a clip. He photographed her right foot – the foot that enters the frame in a high-heeled shoe – she sits there as the room fills with daylight. He photographed her hips; her long legs, which never ceased to astonish Nils. Her blue gaze, slightly out of focus. A cigarette in her hand, and strangely enough it was the cigarette that had shaken Nils the most – not the smoking itself, but that she was sitting there on the edge of the bed with a cigarette, when she usually never smoked. It was as if there were another Marta, one he had no knowledge of, one to whom he had no access. Who was his wife? And who was his best friend? Nils put the photographs away again. He sat still for a while, then clenched his hand and punched the table in front of him as hard as he could. He slammed his fist into the table-top, he slammed his head against the wall, he slammed his knee into the door. He felt nothing, there was no pain in it, he only slammed, thumped, hammered, punched. Flesh against concrete. Flesh against metal. Flesh against wood. He slashed his palm, but nothing ran out. He got down on his knees and pounded wildly at the floor to see whether something would give. That he might sink down through the floors, be swallowed by marshland, by black forest. Fall into the sea, go down in the cold.

THE HOUSE IN VIKA had become a different house. At first, doubt will stand outside such a house; it stands out on the front step, out in the wind and rain. But if you're not careful, doubt can slip inside and start to live its own invisible life, filling room after room. Doubt had crept up into the bed, too – suddenly Nils didn't know how far away from Marta he ought to lie at night, and the warmth that had previously flowed between them no longer reached its destination. Something strange happened to the two floors of their home – they had each taken their own. Marta had the ground floor, while the upstairs belonged to Nils. Before this, she had been the tidy one, he the messy. Marta was constantly having a go at Nils – he couldn't just leave his newspapers and clothes strewn around the place the way he did, he wasn't the only one who lived in this house. Now he kept the upstairs spotlessly clean, so at least some small part of the world was under control. When he came home after having been out on the fjord, he might find the living room full of people, men and women sitting on the sofa, in the chairs, on the arms of the chairs and on the floor, all shrouded in cigarette smoke. On Saturday nights they danced with their hands above their heads and drank wine from the glasses from which Nils drank milk. Some of the men smoked pipes, they had beards and wore square-rimmed spectacles. He'd thought he knew most of the people who lived along the fjord, and a couple of the guests were Marta's friends, but most of them he couldn't place – many of them must be ten or twelve years younger than he was. Nils used to stick his head around the door in greeting, to say hi, hello, before he wandered upstairs. Then he'd look in on the girls, who lay close in the same bed, as if to protect one another from danger. Nils kissed their foreheads, felt the warmth in the room and the warmth of their skin. Sometimes he'd end up standing at the top of the stairs before he went to bed, listening in an attempt to catch something that might help him better understand. He was hungry for information about the world that had now been established below him. It was like a sea down there, mystical and alluring, simultaneously old and new, they danced and swayed like seaweed in the water. The sounds from downstairs rose up through the floorboards, voices and exclamations and songs and bass notes. He could hear a woman saying: *Have we only one season? A single summer, and then it's all over?* He thought perhaps it was Marta's voice, but he couldn't be sure.

One evening, he took off his peacoat and boots in the hallway, found himself a dram and went into the living room. He sat down with the people who had occupied the ground floor of his house. Nils listened to what they had to say, nodding and looking them in the eye. They're bombing an entire people back to the Stone Age, one guy said. It isn't the *South* waging war on the *North*, opined another, it's the *West* waging war on the *East*. Marta chimed in and asked if Nils had taken a proper look at the photographs Robert had taken in Vietnam. Those photographs told the whole story. Marta sat in the middle of the sofa, confident and different, she blended right in, in her jeans and her blouse with an FNL badge pinned to the chest. She smoked and laughed, a kind of laughter Nils couldn't remember having heard from her before. He didn't understand how she could be in favour of those photographs, he couldn't stand them, couldn't bear them. Nils had listened to the arguments all of them put forth, but they didn't listen to *him*. The moment he opened his mouth he was met with a barrage of counter-arguments, before people turned their backs. It irritated him. Because he was, in spite of everything, a man who listened to the radio all day long; he read the newspaper from the front page to the last, he subscribed to both *Life* and *National Geographic*.

The next morning, Nils tidied up downstairs while Marta slept in above him. He cleared away cigarette butts and beer bottles; he knocked the sofa cushions back into shape and sprinkled salt onto red wine stains. When Marta came down to breakfast she was barefoot, her hair a tangled mess. She filled a glass with water, drank from it, stood there without speaking. Nils looked at his wife, the woman who had been part of his life for so many years, and who perhaps soon no longer would be.

Do you think it helps? he asked.

What? she replied.

Sitting on a sofa, smoking and drinking and putting the world to rights.

Probably not, but maybe it'll be a bit easier to live with ourselves if we speak up, show some resistance, don't you think?

Fine – you can be an idealist if you like, but I'm a realist.

You know all there is to know about boats, Nils, but maybe you don't know all that much about politics. You ought to find out more, read something other than that newspaper of yours.

Have you taken up smoking?

I smoke at parties. Why, what's it to you?

I just didn't think you smoked.

You always have to be so *good*, don't you, Nils? You have to do everything right, tackle everything head-on, grin and bear everything – just look at how you've tidied up down here.

So it's better that I make a mess?

I don't know, Nils, I'm just trying to live up to your high standards, but clearly I'm not doing a very good job of it.

Nils paused for a moment. Then he took the glass from her hands and flung it at the wall. It exploded into a thousand pieces.

Is that better? he asked.

She looked at him and shook her head, smiling, almost revelling in his reaction.

Are you going to leave me? he asked.

Of course I'm not going to leave you, she replied.

One Sunday in April, when Nils came up from the boathouse, he found the entire ground floor of the house a flurry of activity. A group of people lay on the living-room floor painting red letters on a white banner; another group was writing slogans in black marker on pieces of cardboard out in the hallway. YANKEE GO HOME, one placard read. SHAME ON THE WEST, read another. In the kitchen, Eli and Guro had also been set to work – they were colouring in the letters on a placard that read: PEACE.

Nils pulled Marta aside, led her down the stairs at the back of the house and asked what the hell she was doing.

You can't drag the girls into this, he said.

Why not? she asked.

You'll get us in trouble, Marta.

How am I going to get us in trouble?

Think about it – who pays our bills?

He was proved right. It's one thing to sit in your own home thinking all manner of things, but quite another to march in a parade in front of the whole village, to act in a way that makes people gossip and whisper. In such a small place, there are certain lines that can't be crossed. Three days after the May Day parade had marched through the village, the old priest called to inform Nils Vik he could no longer employ him as a ferryman. While he had no complaints about the job Nils had done, terminating their arrangement would be in the best interests of both parties. He offered Nils his sincerest thanks for all his efforts.

May I ask if this is about *my wife*? Nils asked.

No, it's based on an overall assessment, the priest said. We're seeing many tendencies to dissolution around us at present, including locally.

I'm the one who drives the boat, not her, Nils Vik protested.

But as you well know, our lives are always illuminated by the lives of others.

In spite of his fears, Nils had felt proud when he saw Marta and the girls walking in the parade through the village, between the houses, past the shops, before they ended up down at the quay. That year the first of May had brought rain and a strong wind, which tore at the banners and placards. The parade was dwarfed, almost consumed, by the immense landscape – it looked as if they might be blown onto the fjord at any moment. How lovely they are, Nils had thought, before a sudden panic had taken hold of him: *She can walk out of our home whenever she likes, taking the girls with her.*

When word got around that Nils had been fired – not just by the priest, but also by the mayor, the district sheriff and the local Conservative party, at least two of whose representatives on the county council were reliant on having access to a boat – something astonishing happened. All those who might have replaced Nils began to call each other up, and agreed they wouldn't ferry these officials around the fjord either. The priest would just have to grab his oars and row himself over the fjord – the exercise would do him good. If the mountain wouldn't come to the great slob, then the great slob would just have to go to the mountain. For the next few Sundays the churches on the other side of the fjord stood empty, and early in June the priest called Nils to say that he had perhaps been a little hasty, it appeared they could now return to the old system. Nils replied that, with a heavy heart, he had decided he couldn't go back to the old system.

Why not? the priest wanted to know.

Well, it came down to an overall assessment, Nils replied.

Oh?

Yes – and besides, my wife is absolutely right. The Americans need to get the hell out of Vietnam.

IT IS NIGHT IN THE HOUSE. It lies there untouched in the darkness, all the rooms grown quiet. Nils returns from the fjord, lets the door gently slip closed behind him, hears only a muted click from the lock. He imagines himself walking through the house one final time, envisages each room, each piece of furniture. He goes upstairs, sneaks carefully under the duvet so as not to wake Marta. He has always loved this simple act, to walk up the stairs and into the bedroom, to see her lying curled up in bed, hands tucked beneath her cheek. Is it you? she asks without turning. Yes, it's me, he says. Where have you been? she asks. Out on the fjord, he replies, and lies down in the bed. He feels the warmth of her bottom against his arm. She turns to face him, opens her eyes. He sees that she is done with crying, that her grieving is done. She receives him, spreads her fingers across his chest, gives to him from the warmth beneath the duvet. She holds his head in both hands and pulls his mouth down to hers, kisses him, looks at him. It's been a long time since she looked at him this way. Nils, she says, my Nils, I'm still here.

NILS VIK HAS MANY YEARS' experience of standing as he is now, straight up and down in the wheelhouse. If you're going to love the fjord you also have to love the monotony, the repetition, the routine; be willing to stand this way for hours on end. Rest an arm on the brass rail under the side window. Distribute your bodyweight between your right foot and your left. Stand on a mat, rather than directly on the decking. Set your buttocks lightly atop the telegraph every now and then. Take in the boat's rhythm, work with the boat rather than against it, accept everything that rises and falls. Follow the seabirds. Listen to the radio, smoke, take sips from your hip flask. Eat a little fruit – it's easy to lose your appetite aboard a boat, but fresh fruit is always appealing, especially oranges. Peel an orange, open it up, sink your teeth into the flesh.

But Nils is disappearing now, he too will soon be gone. All his joints feel loose and unserviceable; his legs grow ever thinner, seem ever further from himself. He yawns and rubs his eyes. His eyelids weigh at least four tonnes each. He blinks against the swarm of blurred shadows out there. The ferries move at their usual calm tempo, back and forth, back and forth. Evening falls, bringing a fresh breeze with it. Seagulls circle the lantern at the prow. The dead have lit fires along the route, surprisingly bright in the darkness. Luna has nodded off – he can hear her snoring, the sound of her claws against the decking. This dog, who once ran through the snow on powerful legs, who rolled around, so young, with her ears flat against her skull. Nils remembers the pure scent of her, her sharp stare, eyes dark as coffee, the afternoons it seemed would never end. This tiny life that passed in an instant.

The radio has stopped working. Have the batteries run out? Has he drifted too far? The radio has always been on in the wheelhouse, playing at full volume, a mooring to the rest of the world. It can't be silent in here – he learned that early on. When terror comes over you in the middle of a storm, you know what you're up against, it's utterly concrete, utterly physical. But when everything is still, no wind, no sound, when the sea lies there like a looking glass – *that's* when you become truly ill at ease. The silence is the cosmos, the great emptiness which cannot be fought, that nothing can be done about. He struggles to open the back of the radio, has only his pocketknife to aid him. He looks over the circuits and couplings, then rescrews the back cover into place, turns the radio back on, waits for the valves to warm up again. The device gives off a warm smell that makes him dizzy. The radio is still dead. Nothing. Silence. A silence that also settles over Nils.

Luckily, Nils can hear the sound of conversation from the cabin. In the cabin his passengers sit, rocked into lethargy by the sea's motion and the hard seats, they stare out of the windows as if at something far off, remote. Jens is there, Jon is there. Robert rests. Kari Aga is there now, too – she sits with Ingrid. They speak together in low voices. It's so good to see you. Are you well? I mean, I'm dead, of

116

course, but other than that. This boat has always been full of talk. Men who spoke about how much rain there had been, or how little. Men who sat with their knees spread wide, the way men do when they don't quite know what to say. Women who spoke in loud voices about children and husbands and who had married whom. Women who spoke in low voices of blue-white scars no one must know about, women who sat here with smiles tugging at their lips, or in silence on their way to operations or abortions. This boat has been full of shouts and whispers, of jokes and the kind of talk that always makes up 30 per cent of the talk aboard a boat – that which is said when only men are on board.

Are you awake? Nils asks.

Wasn't asleep, Luna replies, stretching.

Yes you were – you've been dribbling all over the deck.

Nope, wasn't asleep, just dozing.

Luna says that a face changes in sleep – did Nils know that? The face might grow younger, or the face might grow older, it all depends on whether one dreams forwards or backwards. Nils asks how his face changes when he's asleep. Luna replies that it grows older, because Nils dreams himself back in time, and then his face grows old, especially on the left side.

She looks over at Nils.

But I like your face when it grows old, it looks almost like a mountainside, full of humps and bumps.

His last paying passenger had been the estate agent. Nils finds her name in the logbook: Aud Haver. *Fine August day, almost no wind, temperature around 20 degrees*, it says. She'd had a photographer with her, a guy with a baseball cap and sunglasses, an idiot who had ordered Nils all over the place to get the best possible shots. They were on the hunt for potential summer houses on both sides of the fjord. Aud Haver said the fjord landscape seemed unique and exotic to both Norwegians and foreigners with buying power. This fjord had been declared the world's most beautiful travel destination by an American magazine. She said the interesting thing about a job like hers was seeing how people move and disappear, while property has a much longer horizon, property endures.

At one point, Nils had overheard the photographer complaining about the boat, how they should have rented a better, faster boat. Nils said nothing. He stood at the wheel, staring at the houses along the fjord. People had clung to these hillsides for years, people had done their best, gained ground, and for a while almost anything had seemed possible. But all families, houses, farms, have their time. Then the story becomes another story, or it simply fades away. Buildings no longer inhabited. Doors that soon become impossible to open. Paths that grow over, forests that grow darker. Branches of the fjord destroyed by net pens and fish farms. Hay barns weathered to grey. Outbuildings in need of oversight. Stores that close, schools that shut down. Fence posts that are never repainted.

Nils had hardly ever seen anyone outside the new summer houses. He had noticed the cars that were sometimes parked there, but he had never seen their owners.

In the winter, there were not even any cars to be seen. To the city folk the fjord was a fantasy, a recreation ground, a place that hardly existed until they jumped into the car on Friday afternoon, and which they left again on Sunday evening to return to their lives, where for the rest of the week they would crow about nature and the peace and quiet and the simple life. Aud Haver crowed about it too – what magnificent nature this was! Nils had explained that they didn't say *nature* here, they said forest and rock and mountain and river and fjord, these were things one could point to and be close to and care about, unlike *nature*. He noticed how the muscles around his mouth pulled taut. The new houses were built atop hills and peaks and rocky knolls, they seemed to stick their heads up and shout: Here I am! Over here! Look at me! The old houses lay in dips and hollows, in coves and in shadow – people wanted to protect their homes from the wind and the rain, to save them from time and decay. Those houses were built with knowledge of this part of the world, knowledge that can only be acquired by being here, by staying.

As they approached land that day, Nils had said to the photographer: You know, with the milk comes the cow, and with the cow comes the milk. The photographer had taken off his sunglasses and looked at Nils. The milk? he had asked. Yes, Nils had said. If you want milk, then you have to accept the cow and the barn and the field and the muck, the whole goddamn lot of it. Um, okay? the photographer said, settling his sunglasses back on his nose. We're not cattle, Nils said. We can't be owned.

Surprisingly enough, on that day in August, Aud Haver had invited him out to dinner. His shock must have been somewhat evident, because she had quickly added that she was asking out of pure selfishness – she didn't like eating alone at hotels, and her photographer was heading back to the city. Nils should have said no, because that evening he'd ended up sitting alone at a table out on the terrace. Aud Haver hadn't turned up. It was a lovely evening, the day's heat still hung in the air, music could be heard in the distance, and down by the quay a group of tourists were getting ready to be taken out on the fjord in a dinghy. When they were a little way out the boat increased its speed, and the passengers' shrieks made it all the way back to the shore.

Nils glanced down at his clothes. He had put on his good shirt and light trousers. Luckily he hadn't polished his shoes – that would have been too much. Jesus. An estate agent. What on earth did he think was going to happen? Who did he think he was? Antiquated, ridiculous – that's what he was. A dying breed – time would soon tame him, trivialise him. Nils called the waiter over and ordered a beer. He liked to drink, alcohol made him into a different man, someone who couldn't be disappointed or punished, but right now the drinking made him a man sitting alone at a table for two. But his dejectedness vanished when Aud Haver appeared after all. She'd put on make-up, pinned up her hair. She was wearing a white shirt and a kind of suit cut from red fabric. She looked good. She looked like someone's daughter.

Sorry, she said, I was on the phone to my husband.

I have all the time in the world, he said.

We were arguing – and it takes time to round off a good argument.

What were you arguing about?

Oh, the usual.

She picked up the menu and flicked through it.

Are you married? she asked.

Oh, yes, he replied, I'm married.

Aud Haver asked if he'd decided what he would like to eat. He replied that he usually ordered New York-style rump steak with roast potatoes whenever he was here. She wanted to know if he came here often. No, no, not often. They'd held both children's confirmation parties at the hotel, and their eldest had celebrated her wedding here – she'd married a guy from whom she was now luckily divorced. Nils used to bring his wife here on anniversaries, the big occasions. This was where they came whenever they wanted to affirm the world was as it should be.

Sorry if this is a personal question, but has she passed away?

My wife? Yes, she's gone now.

Do you miss her?

Yes, I miss her.

After they had eaten, Aud Haver said that she and her husband had wildly different views on what a marriage should be. He clearly believed the man in the relationship ought to chase after other women, while a wife's job was to try to stop her husband from doing so.

Nils asked what *she* thought a marriage should be.

Anything but that. It's terrible – to be bound to someone who won't give you what you want.

And that is?

To be loved, I think. Idiotic, isn't it?

But you must have been in love with him once?

Of course – but back then *I* was the one he was chasing. It's hard to believe it now. All I can remember is the sunlight that made me fall in love with him, everything else is gone. I thought I'd remember every last detail. I should have written it down, so I'd remember. Or, maybe not, I don't know.

She laughed.

As Aud Haver added a dash of cognac to their coffees, Nils studied her. All at once he found himself imagining what it would be like to touch her, to hold her, be inside her. The thought arrived so suddenly, so out of the blue, that he almost blurted out an apology. It was just so long since anyone had moved him that way, so long since someone had wanted him, sought him out, craved him. And nobody would ever move him that way again, not like that, not with skin and hair and lust. For him, all that remained was to be undressed, to be washed and groomed and made ready. All he could hope for was warm, gentle hands.

What was your wife's name?

Marta. Her name was Marta.

Tell me about Marta, Aud Haver said, as she leaned across the table and put her hand over his.

THAT NIGHT IN FEBRUARY, when Marta had her first stroke, he had woken to the sound of a glass smashing against the floor. He propped himself up on one elbow and checked the clock radio. A little before three. He quickly lay down again and closed his eyes – he had to be up early. He needed more sleep, he needed all the sleep available to him. But then he had realised that things were not as they should be.

He tried to put his arms around Marta, but she shoved him away and mumbled something incomprehensible into the pillow.

What is it, sweetheart? Nils asked. Shall I call the doctor?

She didn't reply. He went downstairs and made the call. When the doctor finally drove over and examined Marta, he said she'd have a chance if they got her to the hospital quickly. The best thing would be to take her in the boat – all the snow and closed roads meant there was no guarantee an ambulance would reach them in time.

Is it a stroke? Nils asked.

It looks that way.

They supported her down to the boat between them, got her aboard and wrapped her up in a warm blanket in the cabin. As they made their way out of the fjord Nils leaned his head against the side window and saw the snow coming down in great drifts, it was snowing in every direction, the mountainsides were shrouded in white. He tried to memorise what had happened, went through the day and the night in his head, thinking the doctors would want all the details as soon as they arrived. He remembered that she'd felt dizzy the evening before; she'd said she didn't think it was anything in particular, but she had gone to bed early.

Nils sat in the harshly lit hospital corridor until morning, and on into the next day. The local doctor had wished him luck and gone home. At one point Nils went down to the coffee machine in the lobby to get himself something to drink. He somehow managed to make a muddle of it – the cup overflowed and coffee began to trickle down onto the floor – but he was glad of the mess. It meant he could spend some time wiping up the liquid, cleaning up after himself.

He took the lift back up to the fourth floor, sat down on a hard sofa and began to formulate sentences in his head. Everything he would say to Marta as soon he was able to speak with her. All the things he'd never said before, everything he should have told her.

Is she going to be all right? he asked when he finally managed to have a word with the hospital doctor.

We're not sure yet, the doctor replied. She's a strong woman, but it was a major stroke, so she's going be affected by it regardless.

When Nils was allowed in to see Marta that afternoon, there were three beds in the room. She was in the middle one. Her body had been invaded by foreign objects, various apparatus that would measure everything going on inside her. He sat there and couldn't remember anything of what he had intended to say.

The doctor says you're strong, he whispered. You'll be all right.

He said her name, quietly, over and over, as if to wake her, to call her back from a deep sleep. But nothing happened. Her face remained a blank, only her breath caused her chest and the sheets to rise and fall. Sometime in the early evening she began to mumble incoherently, as if she were having a terrible dream. Are you warm enough? he asked. Can I get you anything? he asked. It's me, he said, it's me, it's Nils. She didn't reply. He stared at her hair, which now was grey. He looked at the skin of her arms and thought back, thought about how her arms had changed over the years. Nils sat there with his hands in his lap, as if to make the slightest movement might cause her even more harm.

NILS LOOKS DOWN AT HIS HANDS. They seem huge and old around the wheel. On his right hand is a tattoo of a swallow. Time has caused the bird to bleed across the skin, to become blurred and off-course. He'd had it put there to bring luck, good fortune. He told Marta that on bad days, the swallow made him think of light, of summer. She had scoffed at this – on bad days, she said, he'd surely need more than a goddamned badly drawn swallow on his hand. She had also asked Nils to change the name of his boat, which he had refused to do. You don't just scrape a boat's name from the prow and paint a new one over it, it simply isn't done. And didn't she realise that 'MB *Marta*' was a declaration of love? A name is one's lot, one's fate – a name is the first of all poems, he had said. Even after a person or a boat is gone, the name remains. Yes, Marta said, she had realised, she wasn't a complete nitwit. So what would she rather the boat be called, then? *Day and Night*, she'd replied with a wry laugh. Nils snorted, and said his boat had the perfect name – when he was out on the fjord, on all those days and nights he was away from her, it meant he could still be inside her. You pig, she said.

Luna twists around and stares out through the window. She explains how hard it is for a dog to stare up at the starry sky. Either she has to lean all the way back, as if she's about to howl at the moon – which she isn't – or she has to lie on the ground with her paws in the air, and that just looks silly.

Have we forgotten anyone? Luna asks.

Have they forgotten anyone? Well, of course – most people are forgotten. Almost all of them are gone now. The boat's wake erases days and nights, divides everything into incidents and episodes that are no longer linked. The fjord is oblivion – that's what people don't understand. After the storm, after the accident, after the wreck, there's no evidence. Only the calm blue surface lies there, everything as before, and everything continues, ebb and flow.

There's a 747! Luna says. Up there!

Nils looks up and sees the lights of the plane. It's on its descent, will soon lose its lift, a perfect machine that will find dry land.

Nils? What are those things you used to read in the newspaper called? Cartoons?

Yes, cartoons.

In cartoons, people can have a sort of light bulb pop up over their head, right?

Yes, when they have a good idea.

Yes! Yes! Does that happen, like, for real?

No, unfortunately it doesn't.

But just think how nice it would be if people actually lit up like that.

Luna thinks for a moment.

You're that kind of person, Nils.

No, I'm not.

Yes, you are – the way I see it, you lit the way wherever you went with your boat.

Luna lies on her back with her paws in the air. She asks

whether the people on the plane can see the boat from all the way up there. Nils replies that the plane's passengers most likely aren't looking out of the windows, they have their own busy lives to think about.

But *if* they see us? What will they see?

Then they'll just see a tiny light pulling itself across the fjord.

Has he forgotten the pregnant girls? No, they are not forgotten. The pregnant girls who sat here in the cabin, dark and alone with their secret. He'd wanted to put his arms around them, but he knew he had to leave them in peace, both on the way to the city and not least on the way back home. Nor is the convict forgotten, the guy Nils had ferried one spring day, who said he was longing for his family and life in the country, that he couldn't wait to be home among all the sounds he knew, crows, hens, the distant sound of sheep, the wind, the fjord – but who had panicked as they approached the shore and saw his family standing there on the quay. He'd ordered Nils to turn the boat around and head straight back out into the fjord. Nils had taken the convict to task – he'd said that betraying one's family once was once too often; there wasn't going to be yet another betrayal, not on his watch. The boat was going to dock at the quay over there, make no mistake, and then the convict was going to jump ashore, he was going to get himself ashore and go over to his family who were standing there waiting for him. He was going to walk over to them with his head held high, and then he was going to embrace every last one of them.

Has he forgotten Miss Norway 1966? Of course not. She of the tight dresses and high-heeled shoes, which had made it difficult to get Miss Norway 1966 both aboard and ashore. In the end Nils had found a bottle crate for her to use as a step, which had made life easier for both of them. He'd also dropped a few hints that high heels might not be the best thing to wear when aboard a boat.

I've been wearing high heels my whole life, said Miss Norway 1966. Wearing high heels is about taking pride in yourself.

Of course, and one can only respect that, Nils had said.

This was ten or twelve years after she had been declared the most beautiful woman in the nation and won a Fiat 850. Nils could see she'd put on a fair bit of weight since then. He ferried her around to homes where women gathered to receive beauty advice and order products from a catalogue. Along the way, Miss Norway complained about her hips – oh, her hips were going to be the death of her – and how her sales weren't as good as she had hoped. Nils thought this must have something to do with the fact that this fjord was already full of naturally beautiful women – he was married to one of them himself. In his logbook, he has written of his passenger: *Beautiful people expect so much more from life than life is willing to give them.*

Don't you want to give your wife a nice surprise? Miss Norway had asked on their very last trip. She unscrewed the lid from a jar and rubbed cream onto his hand.

Mmm, smells like a four-stroke engine, Nils had said.

This will give your wife visibly younger skin, Miss Norway said. It's a cream that re-establishes the skin's natural protective barrier overnight.

How much younger will it make her, do you think?

Nils had felt sorry for Miss Norway 1966. Not overly so, but because he thought he could see who she really was. He took out his wallet and bought both a jar of the cream and some perfume. Miss Norway thanked him, then stepped ashore in her high heels. He saw her blue coat, her brown suitcase containing all her products. Then she got into her Fiat and drove away. Nils stood out on the deck for a little while before he went back to the wheel. Then he brought out the jar, dipped his fingers into it, and rubbed the night cream into his face and hands. He closed the door to the wheelhouse, and put out onto the fjord once more.

Has he forgotten Lilly? Surely Lilly must be in here somewhere? Nils flicks through the logbooks, turning page after page. Lilly, who would always take off her shoes as Nils ferried her to and from school. She would take out her pencils and sketchbook and begin to draw, hunched over as if retreating into her own protective shell. You need to buy your girl some new shoes, Nils had told Lilly's mother when she came out onto the quay to collect her daughter, those shoes are at least two sizes too small. The mother didn't reply. She simply looked right through him. Nils had been relieved when he heard Lilly had moved to the city to study at the Academy of Fine Arts. Later, he'd read in the newspaper that she'd had exhibitions in Oslo and Copenhagen and

Berlin. He had cut out a couple of the articles and put them in the logbooks. Where are those clippings? Ah, here they are. At the very bottom of one of the logbook's pages, he finds Lilly. One December day in 1988, Nils had ferried her up the fjord. Lilly's mother was on her deathbed, and in the New Year, after the funeral, Nils had ferried the daughter back to the city. He remembers how on the return journey he'd told her he hoped she wouldn't take it the wrong way, but he was glad she'd moved away. Lilly didn't reply at first, but then she said maybe she'd never really left – she'd simply made it into the Academy and never come back. She explained that her mother had done everything in her power to keep her from leaving. Art was a hobby, her mother had said, art was not a profession, and *artists* were not upstanding people. One evening, when Lilly was fifteen, her mother had gone through all her drawings and proclaimed that Lily possessed not a single shred of talent. She had ripped up the drawings and thrown them onto the fire.

As they approached the city that January evening, Lilly had taken out her sketchpad and shown Nils some of her new sketches. She had drawn her mother on her deathbed, the light casting deep, dramatic shadows over her face. Nils noted the wrinkled, flecked skin, the thin hair, the mouth that hung open – all the years etched into this woman – and death, which was now about to end its work in her. He remembers that he hugged Lilly Gloppen before she stepped ashore. In the logbook, right at the bottom of the page, he has written: *Mother and daughter, two people who only wanted to love and be loved.*

LIFE AFTER MARTA. One October day he walked down to the boat, filled up with diesel, started the motor, found his route. He docked at the quay in the city, sauntered through the streets, found a seat in the railway station café to smoke a cigarette and read the paper. Sometime in the afternoon he took the bus out to where Eli lived. He traipsed around the neighbourhood, pulling his coat more tightly around himself. There were fallen autumn leaves everywhere – they stuck to the soles of his boots. Someone needs to sort this out, he thought, somebody ought to grab a rake and get things tidied up around here.

He stood outside the house, staring at the illuminated windows, as if that would give him information about what was going on inside.

Nothing happened. There was no sign of movement, and nobody came or went. Nor could he see Eli's car. All at once he realised he might be seen or recognised standing there, or that Eli might come down the street and catch him red-handed. He climbed the steps and rang the doorbell. His daughter had looked surprised when she opened the front door.

What's wrong, Dad?

Nothing's wrong.

Has something happened?

Not that I know of.

She didn't let it drop, not even after Nils had been asked inside and served coffee and biscuits. It was as if he'd committed a crime; he was hiding something, he was under suspicion.

You could have called, she said.

I thought I'd just drop by, he said.

Would you like to stay over?

Please.

But you haven't brought anything with you, pyjamas or a toothbrush?

No, nothing like that. But I have my newspaper.

So you just came on a whim?

Yes, he replied. I miss you. I miss us.

Eli said she had theatre tickets for that evening – she and her husband were going to see Ibsen's *The Master Builder*. Had she known her father was coming, she would of course have bought a ticket for him, too. Nils replied that he would gladly make do with watching a bit of television. And if they also had something to drink, he'd have himself a splendid evening. Eli said they had some vodka and fruit juice, at least. Then she went into the bathroom to get ready; she was meeting Tom in the city, straight after work.

Nils walked around the messy living room. Eli explained that they were in the process of redecorating – they were supposed to be laying a new floor, but it was taking a while to get to it, seeing as they were both so busy at work. Nils looked at the books on the shelves. He noted the ashtray on the coffee table, full of cigarette butts. Did Eli smoke now? Or was it Tom? Nothing had ever been said about smoking.

The telephone rang. Eli was still in the shower. Nils could hear the sound of running water coming from the bathroom. He went out into the hallway and lifted the receiver, but said nothing.

Hello? Tom said. It's me. Hello?

Hello, Nils said.

Who is this?

Nils didn't reply.

Is Eli there? Tom asked.

No, Nils said, and hung up.

The telephone rang again, then continued to ring until Eli came out of the bathroom and answered it. Nils withdrew a little, overhearing his daughter's tone out there in the hallway, the way she made irritated movements with her hands. After she'd hung up, she came into the living room and said there had been a change of plan. Eli would take her father to the theatre, while Tom would come home and get started on laying the new floor.

I'm not exactly dressed for the theatre, Nils said.

You can borrow some of Tom's clothes, Eli said.

He went into the bathroom and put on a freshly ironed shirt and suit belonging to his son-in-law. He stared at himself in the mirror. He looked like a different man, as if he'd opened a door onto another universe. He had the air of a politician or a priest, but in a strange way the suit made him feel a pang of longing for something he couldn't quite put his finger on.

After the performance they went for a beer in a hotel bar beside the theatre. Eli said her father ought to wear a suit more often. He looked good in a suit. He looked as if he'd stepped straight out of Hollywood in that suit. She lifted her glass to him and said they should do this again.

Ibsen? he asked.

Yes, she said.

She gently rubbed his arm.

Are you okay? she asked.

Yes, he said.

Do you miss your job?

Yes.

Do you miss Mum?

Yes.

He held back. There were things he wanted to say to Eli, mournful things, comforting things, but he said nothing more. He simply stared at his eldest daughter. Her clear eyes, her feminine movements, the way she said things, the way she laughed – and all the while, he saw her mother. It was all he had now. To other people it would have been nothing, but for Nils it was almost too much.

Eli asked if he had enjoyed the play.

Yes, it was nice.

What did you like about it?

Everything.

He had sat there in the auditorium and watched as Halvard Solness recklessly carried on up there on the stage, the builder who successfully designed houses for others but who was unable to make a home for himself and his family. As the cast recited their way through the three acts, it was as if his own life were being presented under the stage lights – his little life, who he was, who he had been.

He'd felt the blood drain from his face, sure that the audience members sitting around him would be able to see it. That when the house lights came up again he would be sitting there, exposed and laid bare in another man's suit.

When they got back to the house, Tom was slumped on the sofa with a drink in his hand. Eli's husband was sullen and tipsy, he didn't even look up from the television to say hello. He was still wearing his work clothes, suit trousers and a white shirt, he hadn't done a thing with the floor. After Nils went to bed, he could hear voices down in the living room. He couldn't catch the words, but it was obvious they were arguing. Tom's voice was high, almost a falsetto.

The next morning, Nils slept late. There was a note from Eli for him in the kitchen when he got up. *We've gone to work, just find yourself some breakfast. Love you, Dad.* Nils began to tidy up the living room, and then he laid the new floor, centimetre by centimetre, metre by metre; it took him five and a half hours. When the job was done, he took the bus back to the city centre, stepped aboard his boat and travelled home through a dense rain that hit the windows from all sides.

Hello? he called when he opened the front door. Marta?

He knew this house inside out, and yet it was unrecognisable. He stormed through the rooms without turning on the lights, he was shaking, his chest ached, his legs were cold, his mind racing. He swallowed and swallowed, he felt incomplete, so disappointed and sad that tears sprang to his eyes. Finally, he sat down on the sofa. In a flash he understood what a breakdown is, how a life can spin out of control. He went to the telephone in the hallway and called Guro. His younger daughter answered straight away.

Is everything okay, Dad? she asked.

Yes, everything's okay here.

Was there something you needed?

No, no, I just wanted to hear your voice.

IN ONE OF THE LOGBOOKS he's sure there's a photo of him and Marta standing in front of the apple tree in the garden. Nils looks, but he can't find it. It was the American who had taken the picture one Constitution Day – let's see, how many years ago now? Thirty-five? Forty? If he remembers correctly, he and Marta are standing in the middle, each holding one of their daughters by the hand. Marta in her traditional bunad, he in a suit, Eli and Guro wearing fine dresses and new coats. The American has positioned them in front of the tree, so it looks as if they are part of the trunk, the part that's connected to the ground and the soil, and out of this family of four grows a huge tree in full bloom. It's like a snowfall above them, an avalanche, a landslide, snow in May, white blossoms that threaten to come tumbling down upon them. This is also the end of the family tree – neither of the girls have children, despite dragging home one idiotic man after another. No kids, nobody to follow after him and Marta, and now it's too late, this is the last day, time has run out, nobody can go against nature. You can't decide that your daughters ought to get pregnant, Marta had said when he'd complained they would never be grandparents. They don't have time, Nils, they live different lives than the ones we lived. Well, they'll regret it, he had said. They'll regret it, believe you me.

THE BOAT GLIDES INTO the city fjord. Straume. Gravdal. Vågen. It must be ten or ten-thirty by now. The hotels and the buildings sparkle with light. Headlamps roam the streets. Nils Vik has always liked to come down here, to study the other boats and ships, to see the houses lit from within, to see the silhouettes of people here and there, the shops with their illuminated storefronts, and, like now, to hear the sound of the traffic that comes in isolated waves, even late in the evening. Tyres against cobblestones and asphalt, the city constantly changing pace, with its machines and motors and alarms and sirens, the slamming of doors, glasses and bottles being thrown in anger, this low grumbling from the city, the mumbling of the huge buildings.

Has he forgotten Ivar? No, not forgotten. Pushed away, perhaps. Set to one side, certainly. He has held Ivar at a distance, but now here comes his little brother. Here, almost at the very end of his story, comes Ivar. As he approaches the city, Nils finally surrenders to the memories of his brother. Twenty-year-old Ivar, in the back seat of the Opel, making out with a girl – Nils knocking on the window and Ivar turning with a grin. Sixteen-year-old Ivar with a bottle of beer in one hand and his dick in the other, standing at the edge of the forest at the Midsummer's Day party.

Ivar as a twelve-year-old, Ivar at ten, Ivar at five – Nils can hear his little brother whooping and demanding to go higher, higher, as he sits on the swing that hangs from the apple tree. Nils stands out in the meadow on a Saturday in July, barefoot in his pyjamas and hair newly cut, inhaling the scent of freshly cut grass and putrid fjord. He hears the sound of scythes, his father and his uncle sweating over on the hillside. The last of the hay has to be brought in; as soon as they're done they'll celebrate the haymaking with porridge and fruit squash. Nils's head is almost clipped bare – he likes to touch his hair when it's short and spiky like this. Ivar's hair has been cut short, too – their mother has given both boys a summer shearing. Nils is eight or nine, he feels weightless, it's an evening on which nothing can touch him or leave its mark on him, an evening when everything is bathed in the summer light that slowly fades behind the mountains.

Nils slows the boat; reverses into the quay beside the hotel. Ivar looks at Nils oddly once he's aboard, as if he no longer recognises his own brother. His eyes are shadows, merging with the darkness. Still, he holds out his hand.

Thank you, Ivar says.

For what?

For putting me in the ground. I knew I could rely on you. Do you remember how I asked?

Asked what?

I asked if you could put me in the ground, and you said yes, I'll make sure of it, you said, no problem, I'll put you in the ground.

Ivar is both the same and someone else, as if this world and the next have begun to flow into each other. Nils notices how his brother looks towards the window, seeking his own silhouette in the glass.

I didn't mean anything by it, Nils.

No?

You're my brother.

And that means?

That you're my brother – you are. Even though I probably wasn't the brother you wanted.

Did you think of me that day, Ivar?

What day?

You know what day.

Oh, right. That day.

Nils tells Ivar that he went back up there, that day in December. Down on the street he had turned around and gone back up to the apartment, even though it was the last thing he wanted to do. He'd needed to know whether he'd had a chance to save his brother. He had to see if Ivar had packed a suitcase or a bag.

Oh, I don't know, Nils.

What don't you know?

No, I just think we have to accept that we know so little about ourselves.

Oh?

It doesn't help, analysing every little thing.

You idiot.

I don't know what to say, Nils. All I can do is apologise. Would you let me sit down for a while now? In the cabin? I'll go in and sit down for a while. May I?

Fuck you, Ivar.

Nils goes over to Ivar and pulls him close, opening his peacoat and folding it around him. His little brother leans against his chest.

Nils had pushed the unease aside. He didn't have time for it, there were people who needed ferrying back and forth, motors that needed fixing. He needed to get things sorted out first, take care of his own – as if Ivar wasn't one of his own. The unease had never gone away. In these memories Nils wakes in the middle of the night, sure that it's happened. In these memories, he grows anxious every time the telephone rings. In these memories, he stands in the hallway and speaks with his little brother. In these memories, he tries to hear what Ivar is actually saying.

Ivar used to come home to Vika to celebrate Christmas with them. Usually it was fine, pleasant even, despite Nils's little brother always having to say the opposite of what anyone else said, always having to nitpick at everything Nils said in particular. The two brothers were like magnets with the same polarity: they approached each other, pushed against each other, and were then flung apart again.

One Christmas, Ivar began commenting on Marta's appearance. He'd been drinking, and said Marta wore clothes that were far too gaudy, they were almost like the things hippies wore. The USA is on our side, Ivar said. The USA fought for us, he said. When Marta began to protest, Nils tried to intervene. He asked them to calm down, said they didn't have to ruin Christmas over a war that was being fought thousands of miles away. This got Marta all worked up – as if that war had nothing to do with them, she said.

The following year, Marta asked Nils to call his brother and let him know that unfortunately they wouldn't be able to have him over for Christmas. Nils wanted to know what on earth he was supposed to say – was he really supposed to call his own brother and tell him to go to hell? You can tell your brother to go anywhere in the whole damn world, Marta said, as long as he doesn't come here.

I don't think it's a good idea, Nils had said to Ivar on the telephone.

It's my childhood home too, his brother had said.

I just don't want the girls to have to see a drunk in the house.

Nils's brother laughed loudly.

Then maybe you ought to stay away, too.

Ivar said he'd never lost a job. He'd never been in a collision – there wasn't so much as a scratch on any of the taxis he'd driven over the years.

Nils hesitated for a moment, but he just couldn't hold his tongue.

You know, Ivar, the word you're forgetting is *yet*. It's only a matter of time until all those things happen, believe you me – you should never underestimate the danger in denying the facts.

I'm not denying anything.

There was silence for a while, then Ivar ended the conversation. Well, great, he said. Merry Christmas. You enjoy yourself, there by the fjord with your perfect life.

But in the end, Nils had managed to talk Marta round – he said a Christmas alone in the city would hardly be good for his little brother. Marta said there was no way Ivar would ever have to spend a Christmas alone. Many women liked men like Ivar, someone who never gave you what you wanted, someone who'd leave you at the drop of a hat – the certainty that he'd walk out one day would fool many a woman into thinking he was the only man for them. But she had hugged Nils, and said she was glad she was married to him, and not his brother.

On the night before Christmas Eve, Ivar had driven over in his taxicab, a pristine, glossy-black Mercedes-Benz. He sat there behind the wheel, grinning, his nose pressed to the windscreen, gaping at the blizzard. Ivar had brought gifts for the girls, he took Luna out for a walk, he went with them to fish for cod for Christmas dinner, he dressed up as Father Christmas. The brothers stayed up late in the evenings – they didn't drink, but they did everything men do when they're not drinking. They told stories, they played LPs, they made plans, they made promises they wouldn't keep.

On the day after Boxing Day they drove out to the church to visit their parents' graves. Ivar had the side window down, his arm sticking out and a cigarette dangling from his fingers, as if it were a summer night in Atlantic City.

I've spent the best times of my life here, Ivar said as they were making their way back home. Here in the car, alone, when I can just be and flow. When I don't have to think or fret about things, when I can just drive.

Same here, Nils said. Alone in the boat, out on the fjord. When nobody's calling for me, or demanding anything of me.

They looked at each other and laughed.

You can change, Nils said. You know that, right?

Yeah, I know, Ivar said, flicking his cigarette butt out of the window.

Later that evening Ivar got up from the living-room sofa and said he just needed to take a little trip out to the toilet. He padded into the hallway, put on his shoes and jacket and walked out into the darkness. He got into the Mercedes, started the engine and drove the many miles to the city, where he parked the taxi outside his favourite haunt. He later explained that his plan had been to have a drink, a single drink, and then drive responsibly back to the fjord and show everyone he was able to control his drinking. He had changed, he was a new man – he had everything under control. But once he'd sat down on the bar stool that night, he'd understood that a single drink wouldn't prove a thing. One drink, in practice, meant nothing. So he'd ordered just one more drink. And then a third. A fourth, a fifth, a sixth.

The brothers didn't speak for several months. Ivar stopped calling; Nils no longer attempted to get in touch. Nils decided that he couldn't think about his brother any more, thinking about his brother was making him ill, he had other things to think about. One winter's evening the telephone rang, and Nils heard only breathing on the other end of the line. He knew it was Ivar – he could practically hear the way his brother was clutching the receiver, standing there in the telephone box down in the city. Holding the receiver away from his face to hide just how violently he was sobbing.

I'm sorry, Ivar finally said.

Sorry for what?

I'm sorry.

Ivar said his brother had been right all along. *All those things* had now happened. All those things were now here. He had knocked down a pedestrian early one morning, he hadn't been sober, he had injured someone, he'd lost his driver's licence and permit.

And so what do you suggest, Ivar?

I'm sorry, I'm sorry.

Over the next few months, Ivar had started calling manically. He called to let Nils know where he was, he called to go on at length about every little thing he had to do, he called to explain all the plans and ideas and visions he had. Nils didn't know what to say. He listened, he tried to be patient, but in the end he simply couldn't take any more. His brother would have to clean up his own mess. He ended up asking Marta to answer the phone and tell Ivar he wasn't available.

They had no contact for almost a year, right until one August day when Nils had stopped by his brother's place in the city – he'd had an errand in the neighbourhood and rang the bell for the fourth-floor apartment. Ivar looked good. I'm on the wagon, he said. I don't believe you, Nils said. I've been sober for four months now, Ivar said. He said he'd got himself a job at a service station, he spent all day steeped in the smell of motor oil, listening to the radio – he couldn't drive himself, but he could watch the gleaming cars come gliding up to the pumps before they slipped away again. That was enjoyable enough in itself. He also had a new girlfriend, he was sure Nils would like her when he had the chance to meet her. Later in the autumn, Ivar had called to suggest that Eli and Guro might come and visit him – he missed the girls, it would mean the world to him if they came, if he could just be an uncle for a weekend, feel like a normal person. Marta and Nils had discussed it and agreed that while the girls spent the weekend with Ivar, they would stay in a guest house nearby. That weekend, Ivar took the girls to the cinema and the aquarium. They went to a café where they were allowed to share a bottle of cola, and on the Sunday they went to the stadium to watch a football match. When the girls were reunited with their parents, they were beaming. Could they go visit Uncle Ivar next weekend, too?

The brothers spoke on the telephone in December that year, and Nils agreed to go and pick up Ivar three days before Christmas. His little brother had asked if he could stay with them a little longer – he wouldn't mind joining Nils on the boat for a few months in the New Year. He longed for the fjord, he would say the names of all the mountains silently to himself, he said the names of all the farms, trying to put them in the right order, all the way along the fjord until he reached the house in Vika. Nils replied that in that case, his brother would have to be prepared to get up early, he couldn't sit on his fat arse half the day, drinking coffee in his warm Mercedes. Ivar had laughed; said he was looking forward to getting out in the fresh air and sharing a morning smoke with Nils.

I'll pick you up on Friday, then.

Speak soon, brother.

ON THE SHORTEST DAY OF 1979, Nils wakes in the cold bedroom. Snow on the windowsill, snow on the ground. He opens the curtains and looks out across the fragile winter landscape, black trees, grey mountainsides, otherwise nothing but white. He kisses Marta on the cheek and goes to get dressed. A fog envelops the fjord as he saunters down to the boat; at daybreak it clears, making the frost appear thicker, deeper. The snow lies heavy on the roofs and power lines, the branches and telephone wires. When it finally appears above the mountains, the morning sun is dazzling. He docks in the bay and walks through the streets to the apartment building where Ivar lives. He takes the lift to the fourth floor and rings the doorbell. Nothing happens. He knocks, he rings the bell again, assuming his brother is still asleep. It's already after eleven – if his brother is going to join him on the boat, he's going to have a battle on his hands getting him up every morning. Nils tries the door – it's open. Ivar's cat lies on the floor in the hallway. It's been shot in the head and its tongue is hanging out of its mouth. Nils goes into the living room and finds Ivar on the sofa, his body stiff in the well-appointed room. He's exuded a vast stream of blood, there are bloodstains on the cushions, on the walls and the floor. His neck is angled backwards; he stares up at the ceiling, as if he's finally realised how confused and lost he is. His right eye is in the process of dissolving, turning to a jelly-like substance that slips out of his head. Nils backs away, runs down the stairs two at a time and bursts out onto the street, where he crouches down and vomits into the new-fallen snow.

WHAT'S THE BEST WAY TO DIE? No one can know. It's impossible to know. He remembers discussing it with Marta many years ago, after the incident with the elderly couple who lived over on Langøya. He doesn't think he's written about it in the logbooks, but it was so unusual that he remembers it in detail. Malene Myklebust had called, one fine morning in spring. She said that her husband, Gerhard, seemed muddled and confused – her husband needed to see a doctor, she believed it was urgent. Nils had jumped into his boat as fast as he could. Malene Myklebust met Nils down on the quay and walked him up to the house. Her husband, who must have been in his mid-to-late-seventies, lay on the kitchen floor in his blue pyjamas. It was the first time Nils had ever seen a dead man. He'd thought it would be more dramatic – Gerhard Myklebust looked peaceful, the life had simply trickled out of him, as if his fuel tank had run empty. Yes, that's how it had looked, as if the man had no more metres or minutes in him. Nils had gone over to him, lifted his wrist and felt no pulse. Is he dead? Malene asked. Yes, I'm afraid so, I'm very sorry for your loss, Nils said. He gently took her by the shoulders and guided her into the living room, away from the deceased. While they waited for the doctor, Malene said that she and her husband had been together that morning. That was the expression she had used: they had *been together*. She looked down at the floor as she spoke. She explained that it had been such a wonderful morning, with the birdsong and the light and everything. Now she felt guilty, she might have taken the life of her own husband, because after they had been together, he'd gone down to the kitchen to smoke a cigarette, and then he had seemed confused, and he'd collapsed, and now he was gone. What a way to go, Nils had said to Marta once he'd returned home that day, as he sat in the kitchen with a cup of coffee. I'd like to die that way too, he'd said. Maybe not here in the kitchen, but up in the bed, with a hard-on, it would be lovely, just think – to ride a woman like a wave and then pass on. Watch out, Marta had said, I might just take you at your word.

After that first stroke, he had ferried Marta to the city twice a week. He would wander around the area close to the hospital while he waited for her to finish her treatment. Marta walked more unsteadily; the right side of her mouth and right eyelid now drooped. If she tried to smile, her mouth seemed to drop away. She spoke, but her speech was slow, like a record player winding down. Nils had given her one of his unused logbooks, so she could note down what was on her mind. She wrote in large, trembling letters, as if her physical condition also expressed itself in her handwriting. THIS ISN'T FAIR, she wrote. JUST LOOK, I'VE GROWN THIN AS THIS PENCIL. She wanted things to be improving more quickly than they were. She compared herself to the other patients – they were her benchmark, she wanted to make greater progress than the other people on the ward. AT LEAST I LOOK BETTER THAN HER OVER THERE.

Sometimes, Marta would spend all day at the hospital. On these days Nils would trudge through the cool mornings. It was a geography he had learned to love, this city, which unfolded like a sea anemone, wide and waving, street by street, building by building. He walked through the cemetery, reading the names on the headstones. He sat in the railway station café to read the newspaper and gawp at the people who were there to welcome travellers, or who were about to depart themselves. All the men in the city looked like failed film extras, petty thieves, disenchanted Lotharios; the women rushed around as if everything in their lives were undone, they dashed through the day at full speed, in and out of everything that was important. Nils had his logbook with him. He composed sentences he intended to say to Marta, should he manage to pluck up the courage to share them. *You're as necessary as the soil, I need you the way I need bread in the morning, the way I need sleep at night.* He walked over the bridges to watch the winter sun set in the west. He'd been at the foot of one of them in the boat when a Russian circus artist had performed a headstand on one of the cables as thousands of people gasped at the spectacle; the whole family had been with him that day, the girls had shrieked. In the spring he sat on benches and in parks while he waited for Marta. The air was clear, clean, soft. Spring in the city was different to how it was back home. In the fjord the spring brought birdsong and the sound of cow-bells and the bleating of lambs, all the green on the hillsides and in the meadows. Here among the stone and asphalt, you saw spring approaching in people's appearance, how they dressed – thinner jackets, lighter trousers, new haircuts – you saw it in the way the sunlight glistened on the freshly washed cars.

He liked to stop outside the photographer's studio beside the theatre. In the window facing the street hung images of children and newly-weds and familiar faces from the city. The photographer rearranged the display at regular intervals; new faces and new bodies were constantly appearing. Nils studied them all. Despite being taken at a specific moment in time, whether it was in 1989 or 1994 or 1996 – he didn't know, it could have been in 1974, some of the photographs must have been taken several years ago – they had a timeless quality, a bit like the newspapers he collected in the cellar at home: this was right here, right now, but everything still stretched out towards something greater. He stood there, wondering how things had worked out for the subjects after the photographs were taken. Were they happy? Were they still married? Were they still alive? He himself would never end up hanging there. When he and Marta had got married, they hadn't even gone to a photographer. Nils Vik looked at his own reflection in the window. His hair was neatly slicked back. His eyes were blue and large. His face had looked the way it was supposed to look throughout his life. He was sixty-eight. He felt the muscles of his body. He still had perfect eyesight. He still had all his own teeth. He smiled. The girls had come home to care for Marta, but they were actually more of a burden than a help. Can't you be kinder to her? they asked. Can't you do more for her? they said. It hurt him, but he didn't answer, he simply kept on helping, facilitating, doing his best. WHERE ARE MY CIGARETTES? Marta wrote in the notebook, then held it up in front of Nils. He simply shrugged. HAVE YOU HIDDEN MY CIGARETTES? He said smoking wasn't good for her. I KNOW WHAT'S GOOP FOR ME, she wrote. Nils began to laugh, and Marta cast him a questioning look. Yes, I'm sure you do, he said, pointing to the word GOOP in the book. She sat with the notebook for a while, before she wrote: I WANT TO BE CREMATED, YOU CAN KEEP ME IN THE ASHTRAY ON THE TABLE OVER THERE.

He saw how hard she was fighting. He wanted to say it to her, too, tell her she had to keep fighting, but he'd grown afraid of saying the wrong thing, he no longer knew what was worth saying and what he ought to keep to himself. You're the silent type, Marta had said, back when they became lovers. Is there really that much to say? he'd asked. He liked to be around conversation, he liked to hear others chatting, but he'd had little interest in speaking himself, until he met Marta. She had taught him to say the word *love*, she had taught him to say *sweetheart*, she had taught him that if you're silent as the grave, then you're as good as dead, too. Now he didn't know what to say. She grew irritated if he said something she found provoking, like when he had asked what she would say if her ability to speak returned. She had written in the notebook and shown him: I'D SAY: 'I DON'T WANT TO DIE LIKE THIS, LIKE A PARCEL.'

He was a man who didn't like change, he didn't like new things, he had no idea what use he had for new things, he liked that which was ordinary and repetitive, he liked lower case letters and everyday routines. This was far too great a change. The joy at her having survived the stroke was poisoned by his grief at everything not being as it was before, and this nauseating knowledge that nobody survives, not in the long run. It was like the darkness out on the fjord. You become aware of the darkness, and then suddenly it's everywhere.

For her sixty-fifth birthday, he'd wanted to surprise her with dinner at the hotel. When the day came, she had refused to go. She didn't want to sit there on display, she wrote in the notebook, she would not let people see her like this. He explained that everything had been made ready for them. He paused for a moment, then tried again. This would be a day to remember, and the girls would be there, too. PUT ME IN A HOME, she wrote. No, he said, shaking his head, I'm going to take care of you, day and night. PFFT! she wrote. Nils said that she was scaring him, the way she was acting, the expressions she was using – she wasn't herself. He asked whether he ought to call the doctor, he was worried she might have another stroke.

OH YOU'D LIKE THAT! she wrote. I'm calling the doctor, he said. She waved Nils away. He sat down in the chair beside her and said they needed each other – he needed her, too. Without her he was nothing. She flicked back to a page nearer the front of the notebook. PFFT! she showed him again. Then she wrote on a blank page: YOU'RE ONLY LOYAL TO YOUR BOAT. THAT'S HOW IT'S ALWAYS BEEN. He didn't reply. IF I DIE,

YOU CAN SPEND YOUR EVERY WAKING HOUR ON THAT BOAT, she wrote. He didn't know what to say. In the end, he took the notebook from Marta, picked up the pen, and wrote: I LOVE YOU. THAT IS WHO I AM.

THIS IS HOW HIS LAST DAY ends, if you'd like to know. It ends here, with Nils Vik approaching the open sea. The boat has become a night vessel now. The city is behind him; the hands of the clock turn the opposite way, winding as far back as they can go. It's as if his boat begins to illuminate its own movement, working its way towards and into the darkness.

Luna asks how she herself died. Nils says she was run over by a truck. He'd known it was coming long before it happened. The dog had grown slower in her movements and was liable to overestimate herself. She was thrown up into the air, and then she had lain whining and panting on the asphalt for a brief time.

The dog says she remembers none of it. It's all gone. She pads across to Nils, curls up next to him.

I know I was supposed to look after you, she says. But it was hard to do that when I was dead.

It doesn't matter.

How old did I become? she asks.

You made it to seventeen years old.

In dog years, you mean?

No, human years.

Am I ugly? I've always wondered.

You? No. You're absolutely lovely. And you're not all that big either. You're just right. Big dogs grow old so quickly.

But what about you, Nils? How old did you end up being? Y'know – if you'd been me?

Me? Like, how old am *I* in dog years?

Yes! Yes!

Well, I suppose I'm the same age as you.

Seventeen? Are we really a pair of seventeen-year-olds? Ho ho!

The boat glides onwards, outwards, the undulation of the waves is viscous and slow. The clouds part for a few minutes and the moon sends down a glittering light, making the sea appear gauzy and diaphanous before it again sinks into darkness, becoming solid and impenetrable, like thick-flowing tar. Nils sails past the flickering lights of oil platforms and tankers and trawlers. A cruise ship passes, illuminated and over-dimensioned; aboard it are bars, an orchestra, reclining armchairs and swimming pools. The passengers stand out on the deck and wave to him, but he doesn't wave back.

Onwards, outwards and onwards. The sea swells again, its last ebb. He inhales raw air in deep breaths, rests his forehead against the side window, looks up at the night sky. He closes his eyes – just for a few seconds, a little longer, perhaps – then opens them again and feels lost and disoriented. He tries to calculate where he is, he thinks he must be at a latitude of 60.36° N and a longitude of 2.11° E. But he can't be sure. He's a lost ferryman now, off course. He stands there, shoulders hunched, the collar of his peacoat pulled up over his ears. He's disappearing. He's leaving. He sees it on the instruments, he can feel it. He'll be in this body of his for just a little while longer, here in this body, as he has been his entire life. To think of all this body has done, known, felt, made, done again. Soon all that will be behind him. A final swig from the hip flask. A last cigarette, then the time will have come. What will he write on the logbook's last page? He doesn't know. The words escape him, flee into oblivion. He has filled logbook after logbook with his uneven, ragged script. He didn't always know where the words came from, but he wrote them down willingly, with pleasure, as he does now: *South-easterly 5 to 7, moderate to rough sea.*

Nils Vik begins to sing. The boy with the guitar plays, and Nils falls in with the song. He sings. Because there cannot be silence here. Silence wants something from us, demands something of us. Now it's as if his voice comes out of nowhere. It's as if he is one man and his voice belongs to another. Bring them in, he sings. Bring them in from the shadows, bring them in from the darkness. Gather everyone, he sings, bring them down from the mountains, bring them in from the roads, bring them in from the cold and the rain. Gather everyone, drive them down from the fields, bring them out of the fog: collect them, catch them, see them, gather them. Bring me a boat. Bring me a boat. And here they come. Here come all of them. No one can stop the dead, they come from the forest and the undergrowth, they come on foot, they come by bus, they come in taxis, they hang in mid-air above his boat, they become visible in the lantern light. The night boat fills with the dead. Then the radio begins to crackle. A faint voice trickles from the loudspeaker. Nils can't catch what's being said. Suddenly there's a shout. *I'm waiting for you, sweetheart.* The voices simply keep coming. The radio gurgles and spews, breaks out into music and song. Wave upon wave of voices, voices that sometimes glitter before they grow quiet again, the sound of static, snatches of music, the odd rhythm that draws closer, then fades. Slowly, it dawns on Nils that they are talking about him, Nils Vik, and for a brief time the radio floods the wheelhouse with messages about his life.

Ivar Vik: People along the fjord have always viewed kindness as a form of weakness, but he showed that kindness is the opposite of weakness. · · · · · · *Brita Skjeldås*: I never saw him smile, I asked him about it once, if he ever smiled, and then he smiled – You just smiled, I said to him – but he denied it. · · · · *Einar Svortevik*: He was a winter baby, he grew up here beside the fjord, and all that made it natural for him to choose the sea as his livelihood · · · *Fredrik Moss*: He had a good memory, because for a ferryman who needs to seek shelter in a storm or fog, weaving between islands, rocks and reefs, a good memory is worth its weight in gold. · · · · · *Amund Måge*: I ran away from home one summer when I was ten or eleven years old, all I had with me was my goldfish in a plastic bag filled with water. Nils found me in the cabin and went ashore to find a telephone, he called my mother and said he'd discovered a stowaway on board, and then he bought me an ice cream. · · · · *Lilly Gloppen*: He was interested in piston rings and valves and motors, but I think he was even more interested in people.

·· *Margit Jøsendal*: He was a bit like the swallows against the sky, darting here, there and everywhere, stitching invisible threads all across the fjord, holding this place together. ···
Egil Eriksen: One thing most people don't know about him is that he saved a boy from drowning. He risked his own life in doing so, but I never once heard him brag about it.
······· *Jon Anderson*: And he sang so beautifully, yes, it's true, you should have heard him sing. ····· *Ellen Sørtveit*: I met my husband aboard his boat, I was going away to study when I was sixteen, and when I went ashore, Nils Vik told the young man who was also aboard to be a gentleman and help me with my suitcase, and he did, and, well, the rest is history. ·· *Ingrid Alstadsæter*: He was an ineffectual man, and I mean that in the best possible sense – an ineffectual man is a man who makes time for people. ····
· *Robert Soth*: He was a better man than I was, he loved his wife, I always said they lived like two clapping hands, she was the left hand, he the right. ····· *Guro Vik*: I remember his hands, big, strong hands, full of cuts and scars from hard labour. Hands that smelled of fresh air and dirt and the sea. ·· *Luna*: His sleeves were warmer on the inside, he was always new somehow, like, no matter how long he lived, he was new, always very new. ······· *Kari Aga*: He said something so lovely to me once that I had to write it down. He said this life is like an item of clothing, the beauty exists on the outside, but the warmth is found within. ···· *Sjur Mjøs*: I remember he bought himself a fine coat, he always dressed the way a ferryman dresses, but in that coat he looked like a different man, I think he wore that coat because he was

afraid of losing Marta, she was always so elegant, and he wanted to look fine, he wanted her to notice him again, I don't know. · · · *Brynjulf Bleie*: He spent his money as soon as he earned it, that was something you noticed about him, but then again, he probably didn't earn all that much. · · *Finn Tofte*: He practically saved my life, I severed two of my fingers while working with my saw, he jumped into his boat and came to bandage my hand and get me to the doctor, he said I had to hold my hand higher than my heart, I was so dizzy I wouldn't have thought of it had he not said it, all the blood would probably have just run out of me. · · · · · · · *Jens Hauge*: He saw something good in everyone, I think – he cared about everyone, there's so much I have to thank him for. · · · *Eli Vik*: I noticed something at my mother's funeral. As they carried out the coffin, Dad knocked on the side of it with his wedding ring, as if he wanted to say: We'll speak soon, sweetheart.

HOW LATE IT WAS, how late. Nils Vik knew there was little time left to him in this world. Time had dissolved in him, the time that had trickled through this latticework of days and nights. In the window he glimpsed a faint outline of himself. The reflection frightened him – his face had taken on a strange shape, he could see his own skull within it. His face was returning to the fjord and to the sea.

He longed to turn off the motor, cut the power, stop the hollow beats. He wanted rest; yes, a little rest, just a minute – Jesus, just two minutes! – to close his eyes, rest his legs and arms and head. That was always what he most looked forward to after a long day or night out on the fjord. The moment when the motor shuts off and everything falls quiet, the way the calm triumphs over the chaos and the noise, and when you finally feel the solid ground beneath your feet again, you feel at least ten feet tall.

So that was my story, Nils thought. Now he knew everything, now he could see the whole picture. He had come here, step by step, trip by trip. To be born – that is, to live long enough to discover what air and sea and earth and hate and love are, and then say thank you and farewell. This was, in spite of everything, a great tale now – a story with endless outlines and drafts, but a story with an ending, a story about adaptation and acceptance, a story about the past and about change. It's impossible to control a narrative once it's been set in motion. All you can do is follow its telling until the very last second.

When Marta had suffered another stroke one night in October, he realised that death had become entrenched in her, like a mark on the back of a hand or a tattoo on an arm. He could have called the doctor, he could have called the girls, he could have tried to get Marta down into the boat and to the hospital, but it would have been too late, regardless. Now she was fighting somewhere beyond him. Her breathing was irregular, her pulse weak. They squeezed each other's hands. He whispered her name, whispered that he soon would follow.

When he withdrew his hand, his heart was pounding, while her pulse had stopped. Marta turned to him, a kind of recognition flaring in her face, and then it was over. He lay there. He lay there until the light came down the fjord, along the trees. In death she looked as she had looked in life, only paler – how quickly the colour drains from the skin. How could I ever have prepared myself for you? he whispered. How could I ever have prepared for these days, which became these weeks, which became these months, which became these years, which became this life? When he finally stood, he bent over Marta and kissed her cold forehead, determined to remember her every single hour for the rest of his life. It was a promise he had kept.

Now he knew she couldn't be far away, he could feel it, he sensed her presence, in the air, in the rain. He was just waiting for her to come close enough that he could reach out, take her hand, and be led from this world and over into the next. And now here she came, here she was. At the very end of his tale, Marta. She came up behind him, wrapped her arms around him, leaned against him. She put her hands over his eyes as if it was supposed to be a surprise, as if he wouldn't know it was her. He felt her breath against his neck, her tongue moving across his skin. He heard the faint beating of the night in both ears. He turned and looked at Marta. She was wearing her cardigan. She took his face in her hands.

How did you get across the fjord? he asked.

I cycled, of course, she replied.

Over the fjord he went, out towards the open sea, out where there are no more places to hide, where one's legs can no longer carry one, where the boat's heart no longer beats below. Over the fjord he went, he moved towards the light, towards the light in the darkness, the light over the mountains and over the way, over the rain and the clouds and the houses and the horizon. The beginning must have looked like this, a darkness and a light, the darkness with this light in it, like when a boat crosses the black fjord with a lit lantern at the prow. In the beginning he had been a single step from life; now he was a single step from death. Nils Vik closed his eyes, and the last day of his life was over.

In memory of Leiv Grytten.

Written in dialogue with B. S. Johnson, Brit Bildøen, Claire Keegan, Colm Tóibín, Colm O'Gaora, Flann O'Brien, Hanif Kureishi, James Salter, James Kelman, James Brown, James Rebanks, Jenny Erpenbeck, John Berger, John McGahern, Jonathan Coe, José Saramago, Lars Amund Vaage, Michael Ondaatje, Mike Scott, Oddmund Hagen, Ola Jøsendal, Pablo Neruda, Sam Shepard, Sjón, Giuseppe Tornatore, Kirsty Gunn, Kjersti R. Solbu, Erland Cooper, Dag Solstad, Jon Fosse.

Frode Grytten had his big breakthrough in 1999 with the Brage Prize–winning novel *Beehive Song*. He is known throughout Norway for his short stories but has returned to the novel form after more than a decade with *The Ferryman and His Wife*, which was also awarded the Brage Prize, Norway's most important literary award, and his first book to be translated widely around the world.

Alison McCullough is a Norwegian-to-English translator and writer. Her recent translations include *The Widow* by Helene Flood, *Reptile Memoirs* by Silje Ulstein, and *Lean Your Loneliness Slowly Against Mine* by Klara Hveberg, which was longlisted for the PEN Translation Prize 2022.